The Silent Planet

Paul J. Salamoff
Oren Nichols

PRESS

Edited by: Wesley M. Smith
Cover design by: John Leufray
Printed in the United States of America

DEDICATION

This book is dedicated to:

Dr. Donald A. Reed
(1935 - 2001)

Thank you for expanding my knowledge of sci-fi, fantasy and horror.
You left us too soon.

-Paul J. Salamoff

ACKNOWLEDGEMENTS

I would like to thank my support group of family and friends:

Garrick Dion
Jeff Goldsmith
Scott Karp
Neils Olesen
Holly Powell
Adam, Barbara, Edward, & Susan Salamoff
Samantha & Ethan Salamoff
Daniel Schweiger & Penka Kouneva
Christopher Showerman
Stephen Susco
Bill & Brenda Zahn

- Paul J. Salamoff

ΔΔΔ

I'd like to thank my boys, The Bear Lady, David G., and Sammi.
Thanks for finally getting me off my ass.

- Oren Nichols

PROLOGUE
VEGA PRIME

Darkness obscured the dorsal section of the creature as it emerged from the murky depths of the gelatinous Zumerian Sea. As the behemoth slowly rose, gel cascaded off its coarse flesh and rejoined the vast ocean below. Gradually, the shape lumbered toward the shore.

Composed of bizarre tree-like vegetation, the forests of Vega Prime seemed to ebb and flow with life. Deep woods bled into ranges of black mountains scarred by pockets of incredible rock formations and bizarre symmetrical outcroppings. Within the recesses were flickers of small movements, hidden things, and unknown creatures.

Thousands of feet below, a marsh-like swamp teemed with bizarre insect-like creatures and acrid smells.

In a clearing deep within the foul bog lay an object of such immeasurable beauty that it seemed foreign to the rest of the unsightly surroundings. The massive crystal-like sculpture stretched toward the sky with weaving flames of clear resin that joined in its center.

Trapped within the holocaust of symbolic fire was a human man's carved glass form, his hands reaching toward the heavens. The statue's crystal face contorted with agony; its mouth gaped in a silent scream.

CHAPTER ONE

Darkness... Then a loud rapping broke the silence.

Aden touched the lamp on the nearby table, turning it on. He sat up as he rubbed the sleep from his weathered features. A figure to his left shifted under the covers and murmured.

There was another urgent knock at the door.

As Aden reached for a pair of pants balled up on the floor near his bunk and pulled them on, the joints of his lean muscular body cracked and popped. The years had done a number on him. At only fifty-three, he had the demeanor and wear and tear of someone at least a decade older. Space will do that to you. Extended periods of low gravity hit the bones and joints hard, especially if you started in space at a young age. Aden had. Facing the door, he ran his hand through his thinning gray hair and called out to the unexpected visitor. "Come in."

The door slid open, and light from the corridor spilled into the room, silhouetting Panya Bryce in the doorway. The Tech Officer had newly joined the crew and hadn't quite gotten used to how the ship worked. She fidgeted as she addressed her superior. On some awkward autopilot, her eyes kept looking down and away from him and the door opening. "Sorry to wake you, captain."

"What is it, Panya?"

The moving sheets of the bed drew her attention away from her shoes. Aden followed her eyes toward the rustling behind him as a mass of black hair popped out from underneath a pile of thin but comfortable blankets. Samara Lewynn rose from her slumber, her naked body barely shielded by her lover. Twenty years younger than Aden, her age and vibrance were somewhat muted by her acerbic nature and sharp wit. The soft chocolate tone of her skin glistened in the pale glow of the small lamp, and she looked annoyed. "What's going on?" she scowled at Panya. Everything about Samara's demeanor made it clear she was not happy.

The red in Panya's cheeks began to clash with her golden locks and light, almost elfin features. The girl, somewhere in her twenties and apparently untouched by the sorts of things Samara had seen, dipped her head. She was clearly embarrassed by the nonchalant display of nudity before her. "Wade wanted me to inform you that we haven't heard anything from Prime yet."

Aden looked at the display on the wall by his bed. It read 05:24. He was expecting a little more downtime before being pestered by the crew. Unfortunately, this was a typical intrusion from Wade. Wade was Aden's Executive Officer aboard the supply ship *NTSS Magellan*. Aden firmly believed that Wade did it purposely every so often to remind his shipmates of his modicum of authority. He was predictable like that.

Aden let out a wide and unrestrained yawn before turning his attention back to the young officer standing in the corridor. "We're six hours ahead of schedule," he reminded her. "They're probably away from the camp."

"He told me to come to get you, captain."

Unencumbered by modesty, Samara crawled out of bed and headed for the bathroom, throwing her two cents at the door. "Someone should remind Wade that he's no longer the captain. Hasn't been for a while now, as I remember."

Now more awake, Aden resolved himself to the inevitable collision with his XO, "Tell him I'll be there in a few minutes." Panya stepped back, and the door closed on its own.

Entering the small bathroom, Aden headed for the sink as Samara watched him through the clear shower door. Her expression was a mix of pity and sadness, touched with a prick of disdain she dared not dwell upon. He wasn't the only one who had noticed his age catching up to him.

Aden splashed water on his tired face, then tried to stretch out his back. More pops and cracks filled his ears. More than half a life spent at less than the gravity of Earth had changed him inside and out, and the sound his bones made was just one story his body could tell if you listened.

"Oliver's got a bet going on who'll fall apart first, you know," she informed him calmly. "You or this ship."

"Can I get in on that action?" Aden responded.

"Which side are you rooting for?"

Amused, Aden played along. He wasn't blind to Samara's becoming increasingly sarcastic toward him, especially recently. It felt almost like resentment, but that wasn't *quite* it. Or not the whole of it. It was something more profound, more personal. "I'll take the Magellan," he decided. "If I'm wrong, I won't need the money anyway."

Samara continued her shower as she got in one more dig, "She's a strong ship, you know."

ΔΔΔ

The enormous yellow primary sun cast rays of golden light on the tarnished, slate-grey hull of the NTSS Magellan. The mid-sized transport vessel glided through the galaxy like a whale swimming through the ocean despite its bulk. Built in the early 2130s, it had seen a lot of action over the last half-century. The ship had its share of adventures and stories to tell. Its service in the Second Berillion War as a military transport was a particularly rough time for the sturdy ship; it barely escaped the scrap heap after an arc torpedo obliterated the rear engine and most of the aft compartments. If it weren't for the durability of good cargo runners like the Magellan, and a desperate need for more of them, it would have been stripped for parts or left to rot in one of the hundreds of graveyards that interrupt space lanes throughout the Hieber Quadrant. But this ship was different. She was loved and passed down along with tall tales of her adventures from captain to captain, each one making their modifications and upgrades along the way. It was even recommissioned for one fleeting mission during the Mallix Conflict, but the run was cut short when a general armistice was announced only two hours into the journey.

Now retired from military service, the ship was owned by the Gi-Dex Corporation and was part of their supply fleet to the Vega system. In recent years she had found herself in the capable hands of Captain Aden Harker, the latest in a long line of captains that loved her like a family member. Aden had served for a long time on the Magellan and had come to know her every nook, cranny, system, and quirk along the way. She felt like home to him and his crew in the dark sea of space. Regardless of whether the company owned her, she felt like *his*.

ΔΔΔ

The cramped bridge was lined with computers that relied on antiquated touchscreen technology, having never earned the privilege of being upgraded to a neural-link interface or even the bare minimum gesture-based controls. That was the way he liked it. Sometimes it's not worth the money to teach an old dog new tricks, and familiarity bred a blissful contentment for Aden. In other words: *if it ain't broke, don't fix it.*

Leaning over a particularly well-worn console whose

once-sharp corners and clean edges had become more of a series of almost random slopes and grooves, Wade Fassell tightly pressed the comm button with a callused hand marred by what looked like burn scars. Anger and frustration plagued his hard-bitten face. Tall and imposing at 6'2", Wade's physical attributes were part of the foundation of his dictatorial manner and lack of social graces. He was used to getting his way, and right now, getting his way, he was not.

"I don't want to hear any more excuses!" he barked into the ship's comm. "I'll personally tie you to that engine if you can't be bothered to do your job properly!"

"Take it down a notch, Wade." Aden appeared at the bridge entrance and sauntered over to him as he pulled on his flight jacket. "You should know better than that," he scolded his senior officer.

Wade drummed his fingers on the console. "The man's got a problem with authority."

"Who doesn't around here?" Aden retorted with all sincerity.

"Captain, it's the third time this week he hasn't been at his post during routine engine inspection."

"*Respect is a two-way street, Wade.*"

"How am I supposed to take that?"

Aden smirked, "I could have said *there's no 'I' in team.*" He put a hand on Wade's shoulder and gave him a fatherly pat. "So, what's so important that you dragged me out of bed this early?"

△△△

Hair still wet from the shower, Samara strolled down the long corridor that ran along the spine of the ship. She had dressed casually and sipped a cup of hot black coffee. Large areas of the worn corridor walls were scorched and marred with scars and marks. As if telling stories of wars past, the damage to the interior seemed to intensify as she traveled forward. These were old wounds, part of the ship's history and character.

Wade was constantly on the crew about having the walls at least covered up by a fresh coat of paint. It never quite happened, though. That order was consistently avoided as a form of mild civil disobedience on the part of the crew. Something about painting Magellan's wounds, and covering up her history, didn't quite sit right with them. This even included their onboard service mech, who, unbeknown to Wade, was clandestinely reprogrammed by Takashi to avoid any order that involved improvements to the appearance of the central corridor. Her scars served as a reminder that those who didn't learn from history were doomed to repeat it.

A door slid open at the far end of the corridor as Oliver Tross barreled toward Samara. The stocky man with craggy features carried a wrench and huffed at her as he passed. Samara regarded Oliver as he walked away and thought he was the closest the ship would ever have to an ogre on board. Shorter than Wade or Aden, Oliver was built like a small tank, all shoulders and barrel chest. He was a solid guy, a solid engineer, and a grumpy bastard when Wade got up his ass. Samara liked him.

Long familiar with the strained relationship between Oliver and Wade, she found it a constant source of entertainment. "Go get 'em, Ollie," she spurred him on. Normally if she were in the mood, she would follow the Magellan engineer to the bridge to get a front-row seat to the shit show that was about to follow. But she wasn't up for the clash of egos and testosterone today. As she continued her leisurely walk down the hall, she heard voices coming from an open door to the left.

"One more time, Meg," instructed a youngish male voice

with the subtle hint of a Japanese accent.

"Good morning, Takashi," came the reply. The voice sounded odd and feminine but a little off. He was playing with the Mech again.

"No, that's still not right," said the male voice, laced with frustration.

Samara poked her head into the science lab. Takashi Tanimoto sat in a chair, fiddling with a humanoid robot made of white ultra-plastics and black anodized metal. The young man wore glasses and had a scruffy, somewhat disheveled appearance. He reached for a tool and adjusted a regulator within the androgynous mechanoid's chest.

"Don't let Wade catch you messing with the mech," Samara warned him.

Startled, Takashi dropped the tool, and it clanged on the floor. "You scared the shit out of me!"

The Mech's eyes fell on the discarded tool lying at its feet. "Shall I retrieve the driver for you, sir?"

Having worked with Model 5 Service Mechanoids for the past ten years, Samara had become more than accustomed to their monotone voices and irritating command protocols. She had many an argument with Aden over a decision not to upgrade to the new model when they had the chance. He always won the debate, so they got a new linear hyper-injector for the port engine instead. This all went a long way toward furthering Samara's contempt for the oft-malfunctioning mechanoid. It had come as quite a shock for Samara to hear it suddenly speaking with a higher-timbered vocal range that emulated basic human inflection. "It sounds like a girl."

Knowing Samara's feelings toward the Mech and seeing exactly where this was going, Takashi decided to avoid the comment altogether. He bent down to pick up the dropped driver and continued working. "What's Oliver pissed about?" He knew if there was anyone Samara hated more than the Mech, it was Wade. Allowing her to go off on one of her rants would easily keep her mind off what he should or shouldn't be doing to their service robot.

Unfortunately, Takashi was wrong today. Samara was quite interested in what he was fiddling with. She was very concerned about anything that would improve the Mech and make Aden want to keep it. "Same old shit." She took a sip of her coffee and kept an eye on the folly before her. "You know, it's just a machine."

He forced a smile and said, "I know." Underneath that, they both knew that the truth was that Mech was more than just a machine to him. Since Takashi's conception, handled at one of the vat colonies on Mars, he had always been surrounded by some kind of artificial intelligence, mechanoid, or synthetic. Whether it had been his favorite tutor as a child or the one that shadowed him from age twelve to eighteen when he was ready to graduate from Forma-University back on Earth, he had grown to admire their brilliance. They had a simplicity, a clarity of purpose that people often lacked. Takashi saw them as more than just wondrous machines, and he'd grown to love them.

Out of this respect for created intelligences, he made the Mech's repair his primary focus and the improvement of its systems his hobby since he joined the crew over a year ago. Like many of the Model 5s, their Mech suffered from aberrant ticks in its awareness matrix and decision core. This was elegantly resolved in the 6 series, but it was considered such a minor inconvenience to most consumers that many preferred to pay substantially slashed prices for the Model 5 instead. Thus Gi-Dex Corp., being notoriously "frugal," outfitted its lower priority supply ships with the older units to save money. This, combined with their sub-par pay scale and rollbacks on benefits, led to Gi-Dex's motto of *It's all about Space & Time* to be perverted to *It's all about the bottom line.* Takashi had thought about programming Mech to respond with that one-liner whenever it heard the mention of Gi-Dex, but he knew it would send Wade over the edge, so he ultimately didn't do it.

Takashi was also in need of a friend and companion. It's not that he wasn't friendly with the rest of the crew; he just always felt like an outsider. Vat births and engineered humans like him had been given manipulated intelligence that automatically placed them in the upper classes of society and available professions. This led many in the lower-class fields, like the rest of the Magellan crew, to feel that they were marginalized. The reality is that a highly functioning and neurologically fine-tuned brain is only as good as what it's used for — the proof was in the pudding. If being in the upper classes like Takashi secured you a better life, why was he stuck in a bottom-of-the-barrel gig like Tech Officer on the Magellan? Only Takashi knew the answer, and he preferred to keep the skeletons in his closet tightly locked away from prying eyes.

There were speculations by the rest of the crew, most notably by Oliver, who suspected this was some Forma-U study and that the crew was Takashi's thesis project. Oliver was a conspiracy theorist, which often got a chuckle from the crew. As the months dragged on, that theory was laid to rest. Even Oliver knew that people have their limits, and if you didn't need to be in a job like this (even to secure a higher cumulative average on your ratings), you'd give up and bolt as soon as you hit the next dock. This is exactly what their previous Comms Officer had done while they refueled and restocked for Vega Prime over a week ago. If it weren't for Panya being at the right place at the right time (the dock commissary while Aden was doing some restocking of his own), they would be minus a Comms Officer, and Oliver would have had to do double duty, yet again.

The ship-wide comm crackled with static preceding the announcement by the captain. "Samara, Takashi. I need you both on the bridge." He then added, "Bring the mech."

△△△

As Samara, Takashi, and Mech entered the bridge and took their positions, Aden plopped into his well-worn captain's chair. Wade and Oliver stood apart to his right, letting their respective jobs and the magnitude of something unspoken silence their personal feelings.

"Oliver, get back down below and get those engines up," ordered the captain.

The engineer nodded and disappeared into the corridor. Aden then turned his attention to his new Comms Officer. "Talk to me, Panya. Do we have anything yet?"

Panya pressed her headset to her left ear to hear better. Her eyes traced back and forth across her scanner display as she listened for even the faintest signals. "Negative, sir," she tentatively informed him. "Still no response." Panya leaned in over her console and made some adjustments, fine-tuning the interference filters and scanning a broader range of frequencies. She looked at the captain and shook her head.

Having known Panya for only a short period, Aden was still making his mind up whether she was missing something thanks to first-time nerves or if what she was telling him, though highly unlikely, was, in fact, true. He would be the first to admit that he took her aboard on a whim. He had done his due diligence and checked up on her, though—she had attended a fairly prestigious Forma-U for her social class. Luckily, he had a war buddy who worked there and could get hold of him before they shoved off on their month-long voyage to Vega Prime.

His friend had told him that Panya was a bright student, one of his best in years, and had left Forma-U with high honors—leading some to wonder if she'd had any neurological adjustments done. This was superfluous to Aden, who took on new crew members based on their likability and temperament more than anything. Most monkeys, modified or not, could run the comms board. You might as well bring one you're going to get along with over long periods rather than one who's too uptight about the job. Heavens knew Wade had a stranglehold over *that* personality type already.

Panya wasn't too hard on the eyes either, and it was about damned time they had a little more estrogen aboard the Magellan. Especially given how Samara had transformed in recent years. Samara had always wanted to be one of the guys and, unfortunately for Aden, was excelling too much in that area. It wasn't that their sex life was terrible; it had its typical ups and downs like most relationships. It was that it had become more about aggression than anything resembling love or lust, and that stood out to him. Things had changed, grown almost feral over time, between them in the bedroom. Once slow and sensual, her scratches on his back were now more prone to making him bleed a little. Having someone like Panya, whom Aden could clandestinely ogle, would be good for him and thus good for the crew. Mission accomplished.

Aden decided to push her a little to test her. "I was told you're quite the comm whiz kid, Panya," he prodded. "That's all that you've got for me?" Panya was more than a little pink and too flummoxed to reply, so he turned his attention to Takashi, who was now strapped into the pilot's seat.

"Takashi, double-check our position and convince me we're not jumping the gun here."

"Aye, sir," replied Takashi.

Aden turned to Mech, who was positioned by the Magellan's datalink port. As the robot's left hand unfolded and transformed, it revealed a grooved metal rod that slid smoothly into the port on the console before it. It interfaced directly with the ship's systems, all of them, and in its digital way, became one with it. Mech was now the ultimate central interface for the Magellan, giving the captain and his crew more flexibility to focus on the situation at hand.

One of Aden's frustrations with the Mech and Takashi was that the damned thing's high-speed wireless was burnt out and had been for some time. This was particularly problematic when doing diagnostics and repairs of the individual systems aboard. Mech would have to go with them to each terminal during these monthly maintenance runs, and, given how cramped the Magellan was, the more was not the merrier. After a while, Aden started sending Samara in his place to assist Oliver just because she was physically smaller.

Aden spoke methodically to the mechanoid so it would understand his request the first time he asked. "Mech, compile astrometric data on the surrounding area. Pay particular attention to solar flares or anomalous interference that could prevent us from hearing a transmission from Vega Prime."

"Affirmative, captain," replied Mech in its modulated feminine tone.

Bewildered by the female flavor of its speech, Aden turned to Samara for an explanation. "What happened to its voice?"

Samara gave an accusatory nod toward their Tech Officer. "Ask Takashi."

Business first, Wade stepped up to Aden and gave his assessment of the current situation. "Captain, we are definitely in comm range."

"I just want to be sure." He turned back to the mechanoid. "Mech, is there any quantifiable interference?"

The answer was instantaneous and definitive. "Negative, captain."

"Something's wrong," said Takashi. "I know it."

Getting up from his chair, Aden crossed to the communications station. He was growing concerned, and it was worth being sure before Plan B would be put in motion. "No word yet?"

"Nothing, Sir," Panya answered.

Aden nodded. Time for Plan B: kick it up the chain. "Patch us through to headquarters."

CHAPTER TWO

The Magellan set course for an enormous ringed planet silhouetted by the primary sun of the Vega System. Rounding a small moon, it came face to face with Vega Prime. Even in the distance, it was somehow imposing. The earlier survey and research teams had found many things about Vega Prime anomalous. One of its most interesting features was its gravity, close to Earth's normal for such a sizeable stellar body. Though several had been proposed, no explanation for this had yet been settled on. Takashi pondered this as the ship drew closer.

Seated in his chair, the captain stared at the main viewscreen displaying Vega Prime looming in the distance. An inset sub-screen appeared in the top right corner of the wide rectangular monitor at the front of the bridge, displaying the Gi-Dex corporate logo. The logo faded, and O'Neil appeared unstressed and unconcerned, typical for a man unfettered by life-threatening situations that unfolded in real-time. He was corporate through and through, a real "company man." Toeing the line was not an option but a way of life for the Senior Gi-Dex Representative for the New Look Consortium.

Petty concerns always had a way of getting under O'Neil's skin. The annoyance today was Captain Aden Harker's anxiety that there might be something amiss because they had not heard from the survey team on Vega Prime since entering comm range. It was O'Neil's responsibility to ensure things ran as smoothly as possible. He was in charge of a whole floor of accountants, and he'd felt for a couple of years now that the Vega Prime project was straining the bank as well as the patience of the Board.

He could barely care less—what was the problem? The team on the ground was probably off doing their damned jobs while Harker raised the alarm over what was probably nothing.

"Mech performed an all-frequency sweep for a distress beacon," informed Aden. "But came up empty on that as well."

"Exactly," huffed O'Neil, barely masking his annoyance. "Why would there be a distress beacon? Those guys have better things to do than check in with us. We leave them alone for long periods to do what they do. They're not used to contacting us unless something comes up or they need something."

"You said it's been over a month since you last heard from them." Aden reminded him.

"So what? I remember when we'd hear from them *every day*," he retorted. "Now we consider ourselves lucky if we receive their bimonthly report."

The captain shook his head. "Something just doesn't feel right."

Aden was pushing his buttons. "Captain Harker, you're getting paranoid in your old age," he said bluntly. "In the six years they've been wasting the Corporation's money on this idiotic project, there has been not one incident."

Having had enough of the company man, Samara stepped up to the viewscreen to make sure O'Neil got her tone. "What about McMasters?"

By his change of expression, it was clear that she had made her point. "That was two years ago." he fumed back.

Confused, Panya turned to Takashi. Her look said it all: *what are they talking about?*

Keeping his voice down, Takashi summed it up as concisely as possible. "He was a member of the survey team. He went native. Ran off. Nobody knows what happened to him. Rumors the planet drove him crazy somehow."

Knowing so little about Vega Prime, Panya couldn't understand the ramifications of that statement. She just nodded and resumed listening to the ever-increasingly contentious debate.

Aden had his theories on McMasters. Having served for years as a Corporal in the general army of the United Organization, he had seen many soldiers go AWOL from the intense pressure. A particular Private named Thad Brinner inexplicably went absent during an extended lull in the fighting during the later years of the Mallix Conflict. Their Troop Commander speculated that Pvt. Brinner went stir-crazy because there was no one to kill, and that's what he had been trained to do (or brainwashed to do, depending on who you asked).

This was confirmed when the deranged Private returned a week later and waged a one-person assault on their barracks that lasted over forty-eight hours. Pvt. Brinner was so well trained that he was able to take out half the company before he was slowed by a thermal grenade that ultimately caused more damage to the remaining troops than to him. He, unfortunately, didn't succumb to the wounds inflicted by the grenade. It was a point-blank bullet fired into his skull by Cpl. Aden Harker that finally squelched the fire of insanity. So, in this regard, Aden had first-hand reason to be wary of what can happen in situations of high stress and isolation while facing uncertainty or the unknown. "What if McMasters came back?" he postulated. "They never found him."

"They never found him because he's dead," O'Neil spat back at him. He was done with this ridiculous discussion and decided to end it once and for all. "Now, do your job and report to me after you've dropped off the supplies." This was an order, not a request, and his tone made it very clear. "O'Neil, out." The corner of the screen immediately went black as O'Neil abruptly ended the call.

There was a moment of silence on the bridge of the Magellan as the Gi-Dex logo replaced O'Neill on screen. Nobody appreciated being talked to like that, especially when they had a legitimate concern. This was par for the course in dealings with upper management. It looked like the Magellan, and her crew, were on their own on this one. Hopefully Aden was wrong, and the truth was that the survey team had just gotten lazy.

As if Samara had read his exact thoughts, she leaned in close and spoke her concern. "We're not equipped for search and rescue."

Aden drummed his fingers on the armrest of his captain's chair as all the bullshit problems this situation could present flitted about his brain.

△△△

Up until now, the crew of the Magellan had a particular and routine job: bringing supplies every two months to the survey team on Vega Prime. It couldn't be more cut and dry. Load up and refuel at Dock 85a by Jepaas, then make the three-and-a-half-week trip to Vega Prime. They would contact the survey team as they got close, then land at the ground port, where they would be met by one of the team members who arrived via their land skiff. It was typically Dr. Zimmerman (except for the two random times it was Dr. Archer). No one from the Magellan would even step off the ship. The skiff easily docked with the rear platform of the Magellan, and the items were passed from one hand to another. This was all done in the safe confines of the rear hull.

After some very minor gossiping about current events, Dr. Zimmerman would head back to base camp and the Magellan would leave, ready to start the process again. It was mundane and repetitious, but this is the way they liked it. When Samara hinted at a potential search and rescue scenario, it caused Aden to tense up immediately.

Samara didn't need to see the vein bulging in his forehead to get the picture. She knew Aden well enough to let him have his space for now. "I'll see what I can put together."

CHAPTER THREE

As the massive sphere of the planet filled the screen, the view began to reveal the surface of Vega Prime. Burnt reds and charcoal blacks splotched the vast green and yellow landmasses that came into view as they approached. These were separated by a mild greenish-blue ocean known as the Zumerian Sea.

The Magellan held its course as it dove through the upper atmosphere. The crew worked diligently at their posts, keeping the bulky vessel on its flight path. Sporadically the ship would lurch, tossing the bridge crew around in their seats.

"Angle steady, but atmospheric shear is up twenty-three percent," informed Takashi as he kept them on course. His skills as a pilot were good, better than most. Takashi's advantage in the pilot's chair was his fine-tuned neurology. His reaction times were so fast that sometimes his moves seemed preemptive. He was good at flying, and he liked it.

"Decrease angle to compensate," instructed Wade unnecessarily.

Takashi always hated this part. Nothing can describe the experience of tearing through the atmosphere on approach to a planet. The only remotely comparable thing would be if you were tied backward and upside down on the world's fastest roller coaster. This, however, was a minor inconvenience compared to what Takashi spied on his flight computer monitor. "We're going to hit a super dense spot..." he said, and his words were tinged with an uncharacteristic note of concern.

Wade looked to the captain, who nodded. "Hold the

course," commanded the XO.

"OK. But it's going to get bumpy."

Everyone on the bridge took that as their cue to ensure they were secured. A gust of white engulfed the viewscreen not a second later, and the Magellan began to rumble, then shake. It seemed as if it were poised to stop for a moment, then the ship lurched all at once to the side and down. For as hard-assed as he liked to think, Wade almost lost his lunch.

"Keep that nose *down*," Wade yelled at the young pilot.

The stick in Takashi's hand bucked and suddenly pulled from his grasp. "Shit! This turbulence is *nuts!*"

Wade's tolerance for Takashi's whining was at an all-time low. "Welcome to Vega Prime. Now get it together!"

Takashi lunged for the stick. It took all his strength and considerable dexterity to stabilize it. Wade appreciated what the man was going through and how good at the job Takashi was, but he was in no mood to die because the pilot was whining about atmospheric conditions instead of flying the damned ship.

Sometimes feeling the necessity to counter Wade's gruffness, Aden decided to chime in. "You're doing fine, Takashi. Do what you need to do. I trust you." This had the side effect of seeming to annoy Wade even more. Aden had become something of a mentor to Takashi in their time together, which also bugged Wade. Aden didn't care.

Aden's philosophy was that you "got more with honey," as the old saying went, which extended to his command style. It was great to have a hard-ass XO like Wade Fassell because everyone directed his or her hatred toward him, while Aden got to be the good guy. It suited Wade. They split the heavy lifting, but in the end he relished the authority in a way that Aden didn't. It suited Aden too. While everyone was pissed off at Wade, he could do no wrong in the eyes of the crew, and that included his relationship with Samara.

Submerged in the dense opalescent cloud, the large transport vessel banked to the left as it descended toward the surface. Billowy white with strange tinges of blue and yellow hugged the sides of the hull like a shroud and then burned up in the ship's exhaust. It didn't reasonably behave like water vapor. Takashi wasn't sure *what* it was, but he was too busy flying through it to work that out.

Aden held on tightly to his seat as the vibrations continued to rock the vessel. His eyes focused on the obscuring clouds searching for the skies of Prime.

Red emergency lighting suddenly flooded the bridge as the clouds dissipated, and a warning klaxon blared. The forward proximity alert sounded. They broke through the last of the clouds, and a large mass appeared directly in their path. A mountain of yellow flesh filled the viewscreen as Aden's eyes grew wider. "Turn! Turn!" he yelled to his pilot.

Takashi had no time to maneuver. He altered course, tried to make a quick hard shift in their approach to dodge, and didn't pull it off. The port side of the ship struck the huge mass along its bulk, the two dragging along each other. It took everything he had to keep the ship from going straight down as it peeled away, and he almost burned the engines on that side to a crisp doing it. "We've hit a drifter!" he shouted as chaos erupted on the bridge. They were heading straight for another of the floating masses.

Wade unbuckled himself and raced over to a control panel nearby. "There's more than one." His eyes widened in fear, awe, or a mix of both.

An entire pod of Drifters surrounded the Magellan. The ship had dropped into the atmosphere and descended right inside a cluster of them. These massive airborne creatures had a yellowish hide and were roughly the size of one of the bigger cargo haulers the crew had seen. Shaped almost like giant snails, they hung in Prime's sky and drifted along using the wind currents of the middle atmosphere to float on. Their bodies were rounder and bulbous at the rear, where huge sacs of trapped gases lighter than the rest of the atmosphere pulsated below the surface. These sacs and the internal gills that filtered the gases as they entered them stretched and pulsated — expanding and gathering more, contracting and venting to assist in their thrust and navigation.

This pod consisted of about twenty of them in an elongated diamond-like formation. The Magellan bobbed and weaved as best it could between them as they moved about, trying to avoid another collision. Samara and Oliver burst onto the bridge and saw the massive shapes on the viewscreen. Aden was too busy pouring over instruments and readouts to notice their arrival as he tried to deal with the surmounting chaos. "Mech! Turn off the goddamn sirens!"

Mech, already jacked in, sent the proper commands. The wailing of the klaxons stopped immediately.

Finally able to concentrate, Aden turned to his frazzled pilot. "Takashi, slow us down."

Sweat beaded on Takashi's forehead as he adjusted the forward and rear engine throttles, then resynchronized his means of propulsion. The engines at the front of the ship were mounted on either side and rotated slightly upward in response to his control changes. The hull tipped up slightly for a moment, and the increased drag, coupled with the decreased power to the engines, slowed them abruptly. The crew that was seated lurched and the crew that was standing was nearly knocked down. The ship steadied and leveled out.

"There's got to be over twenty of them..." surmised Oliver, still standing before the viewscreen in awe as more came into view. Next to him, Panya stared transfixed, frozen in fear. Aden continued to belt out instructions to Takashi. "*Pace them*, Tak."

Sensing Panya's distress, Samara crossed over to her with the thought of calming her down. The last thing they needed right now was another situation to take care of — let alone drama from the new kid.

Panya looked like a child, scared of the monsters lurking under her bed. "Are they going to *attack*?"

Samara felt for the girl. The first time you see a drifter, she thought, it can be hard to comprehend -- especially the size of one this close. *Her* first time, Samara had had a completely different reaction. The awe at the creatures' sheer massiveness and graceful motion left her with a feeling of wonderment and a sense of adventure. That was years ago when she was far less cynical and more hopeful for the future. These days Samara was doing something more like marking time.

"We don't know," she offered calmly. "I don't think anyone's ever been this close to a Drifter. At least not intentionally."

Wade checked the set of readings on the command screens one more time. He shook his head, frowning. "Captain, I don't think we can safely maneuver through...."

"Watch out! They're turning!" Aden suddenly yelled at Wade and Takashi.

The Drifter to the port side abruptly cut in front of the ship and released a nearly spherical glob of what looked like some sort of green gel from an orifice on its belly. It was unfolding, *unfurling...* part of it split and spread apart in a display reminiscent of a giant gelatinous butterfly. The viscous substance lobbed from the massive beast and hammered against the hull of the Magellan like a stream of thick mud. The ship recoiled and rebounded, vibrating from the impact. Everyone retook their seats and strapped themselves in.

Aden turned to Oliver. "Engines?"

"Peak operating, Sir. Can't squeeze much more out than Takashi already has, but they're solid."

"Hope you're right." With that, Aden focused his attention

back on Takashi. What he said next was almost too insane to believe.

"Cut 'em off! Cut the engines!"

Takashi turned to Aden with a look of doubt on his face. He couldn't be serious.

Aden was quite serious. He did not intend to die today and gave Takashi a reassuring nod.

"Trust me." He said as their eyes met.

The pilot's hand hovered above the bank of thrust and engine controls as Aden continued.

"You better be ready to hit it hard and go for a controlled burn on my word."

Aden turned to the rest of the crew and told them to hold on to their asses, but they were already ahead of him. Everyone was holding on for dear life already. They had all gotten the message. Taking a deep breath, quite possibly his last, he thought, Aden nodded to Takashi.

"*Do it.*" Said Aden. Takashi nodded and tensed a little.

Covered in slowly spreading green bile, the Magellan was moving between two Drifters. Suddenly the engines cut out, and the hum of power flowing to them ceased. There was a moment of almost peaceful stillness as the ship hung in the air flying free with the Drifters. Then, not a moment later, the ship plummeted like a rock.

Just as it was about to clear the herd, a smaller Drifter shifted its position and glanced off the hull of the falling vessel. The transport ship was no match for the inertia of the behemoth as it skidded along the ship's belly and turned away, causing the ship to spin like a top.

The Magellan tumbled toward the planet's surface in a spin. If Takashi couldn't get it under control, there wouldn't be much left of them. Inertia was building fast, making everything worse for the pilot as it became harder and harder to counter the ship's movements. As if that weren't enough, it had begun to roll – that would create one too many variables for Takashi to compensate for. This was the worst situation he had ever been in, trying to right this unwieldy hunk of metal falling through space. The sudden G forces plastered everyone in their seats. Warning lights flashed on at every station illuminating the cabin and the terrified faces of the crew in red. On the viewscreen, the surface spun faster as it approached.

Aden strained to open his mouth, held tight by the intense pressures. "Engines! *Now!*"

Takashi gripped the panel and slammed his hand down repeatedly on the button that engaged all the engines at once, but nothing happened. He checked the synchronization controls and main thrusters, then the secondary thrusters. Things were responding, but they were doing it out of sequence, which would only worsen their situation. That kind of instability in motion at speed could rip the hull apart, and from where Takashi sat, this was a clear possibility. Aden recognized this too.

"Tak!!!"

"It's not working!" screamed Takashi, his eyes wide with panic.

"It's the injection coils!" piped in Oliver. "Keep trying to sync the coils — rapid pulses!"

Takashi did what he suggested, slamming the sync button with one hand in short bursts. The other hand was poised over the engine start control, ready to ignite their thrusters as soon as they were prepared. Watching a small readout above the sync controls, Takashi saw the main engines get closer and closer to an ignition state. It felt like it was taking hours. He started slamming the ignition button out of fear and panic, losing his cool.

Panya began to lose consciousness from the G forces and

abrupt, randomized motion in the cabin. Her head slumped forward, repeatedly bashing against the comm equipment as the ship spiraled out of control. There were little drops of blood on the keyboard at her station, blending with the red glow of warning lights. In her unconsciousness, she had hit her nose and upper lip. She hadn't sustained any overt damage, but she had a nosebleed.

Takashi pounded on the ignition button harder and harder out of sheer terror, slamming it until his hand split and blood began to flow from the wound. As if the ship had received a sacrifice, the button lit up, and the roar of power filled the bridge. Instinctively he grabbed the flight stick and tried to regain control of the Magellan. The ship was coming out of its spin thanks to Takashi's reflexes and Oliver's prized stabilizers as it raced toward the surface. It wasn't happening fast enough -- the burst of power had thrown the ship forward harder than any of them had anticipated.

"Oliver, override the forward engine safeties. Flip them like it's an orbital retro burn." Aden said. Oliver looked over at him like he was crazy. "Do it!" said Aden. They were almost out of time.

Just miles above the rocky terrain, the forward engines slowly rotated so they would fire backward, acting as powerful retro rockets. They weren't intended to do this in the atmosphere or to be rotated at speed, but Oliver had his orders. Aden and Takashi both knew standard retro rockets would not help them anymore. This was a Hail Mary. Oliver prayed the struts the engines were mounted on would hold.

Aden leaned forward, flushed with adrenaline. "Pull up and fire forward engines and hull retros."

Takashi grabbed the flight stick, now slick with his blood. He yanked it back with all his might as the ground began to disappear from the viewscreen, then he slammed two more controls on the console with his fist. The ship jerked as it slowed, and the hull vibration slowly faded.

There was a collective sigh of relief. With a slight smirk on his face, Aden turned to Samara. "Now, are you glad we got that new linear injection coil for the main engines?" He loved being right, especially after a crunch.

Still reeling from the wild ride, all Samara could muster was to flip him off, which Aden took as a sign of his victory.

"Classy." He winked at her before turning to Oliver. "So, Oliver, does this little escapade impact the odds in my favor in your damned betting pool?"

"I'll check with my bookie." Oliver smiled back, sweat still evaporating off his brow. The Engineer admired the captain. Anyone who could joke around mere minutes after near annihilation deserved his respect.

As Samara unstrapped herself from her seat, she saw Panya slumped over her console. She raced to the younger woman's side and brushed the hair from her face. "Panya?" She was either out cold or dead. "Panya, Wake up!"

All eyes fell on the source of the urgent sound of Samara's demand for a response. Her fingers went to Panya's throat to check for a pulse, but as she did, the young girl moaned softly and began to stir. As Samara unbuckled her comrade, she turned to the XO. "Wade, give me a hand."

CHAPTER FOUR

The woefully small infirmary barely had enough room for the ship's medical technician and a single patient. Lined with shallow cabinets sunken into the walls and recessed pullout drawers, it did make fine use of its lack of space. Anything that could be folded away, stacked, or made retractable was. The place was organized and spotless compared to the rest of the ship. You could tell it was Samara's dominion and Samara's alone.

Slightly dazed, Panya lay on the single examination bed. Sensors, placed at multiple points on her body, connected to various diagnostic systems and a bank of monitors embedded in the wall to her left. She looked nervous. "I must have just passed out from exhaustion…I haven't been sleeping… or eating much…" she admitted with a look of guilt on her face.

Samara studied the readouts as Wade looked on. Her expression stayed stone-faced as she noticed something on one of the viewscreens. If the data from the reading were correct, then it would be best if Wade wasn't present. "I can take it from here," she informed the XO.

He nodded, eying Panya with a look of annoyance. "I'll expect a readiness report before she's back on the bridge." He exited, relieved to be out of the cramped space. Forgetting his reactions moments earlier, he thought he had better things to attend to than a green crew member who couldn't handle a spot of turbulence.

From the instrument panel, Samara removed a small wireless handheld device. Placing it on Panya's belly, she looked at the readout. Confirming her suspicions, she replaced the scanner in its holder. "Do you want to keep it?" she asked in a detached, clinical tone.

Panya rolled on her side away from Samara. "I don't know," was all the terrified girl could muster. And this was the truth. She *didn't* know. She hadn't decided whether to abort the baby, see it through, or at the very least half-term and then transfer it to a pre-born adoption agency for the rest of its gestation. The only thing she did know was that she didn't want her parents to find out. It was for this reason that she jumped at the chance to join the crew of the Magellan. She could get away, escape her worries, and have the time to sort it out. At least, that was her plan.

The baby's father was a frequent visitor to dock 85a. They had a fling that ended a few weeks before she left for Vega Prime. He had his head in the clouds, always talking about being the next great Striker Pilot for the United Organization Task Force. It was a pipe dream considering that he was unmotivated to do more than talk about it and wasn't an outstanding pilot. Right after Panya met him, he was demoted to co-pilot of the garbage scow he had been working on for the last four years because he had repeatedly smashed it into the docking bay platform, causing hundreds of thousands of credits in damage.

None of these flaws mattered to Panya in the beginning. Jason was beautiful. He had a great body and smelled great for someone who worked with garbage all day. His scent was almost intoxicating to her, and she could bury her head in his chest and get lost in it when they were cuddling after sex. It made her feel safe. He knew his way around her body and how to attend to her needs and desires in a way that made her feel special. Unfortunately, like most relationships based primarily on physical attraction, theirs didn't last long.

Panya needed to be free, connect, and feel love, romance, passion, and lust. Having lived under the oppressive thumb of her overly strict parents, who were devout Universalists, she sought ways to express her independence when she met him and felt like she was still finding it even after they broke up. Then she discovered she was pregnant. The birth control she was taking failed her and gave her the misconception that it was normal to be missing her period.

Panya was still reeling from the idea of pregnancy when the opportunity to join the crew of the Magellan presented itself. She thought the long journey might give her the time to sort her head away from her controlling fundamentalist parents. She was hoping to keep her situation to herself. It certainly didn't help that her petite frame made hiding her growing belly a daily challenge. What she thought would be a run-of-the-mill supply drop had suddenly taken a left turn, much like her life -- and it had smacked her in the face with the unpredictability of reality. This frightened her and filled her with doubt. Maybe terminating the pregnancy here and now would be in her best interests before it became a problem. Her head was swimming as she turned back to Samara. "I don't think I'm ready for this."

It honestly didn't matter to Samara what Panya decided to do. It was the younger woman's decision. She was only there to facilitate. "Well, I wouldn't wait too much longer to decide," said Samara as she removed a small, sealed package with a warning label from one of the tiny nearby compartments. She looked the package over, then handed it to Panya. "Should you choose to terminate, you'll need these. I'm giving them to you so you can choose your own, privately, without any outside pressures. I want you to be sure, and I want you to be safe." Panya nodded at Samara as she continued. "If you choose to use these, take the first pill on an empty stomach. It will preload your reproductive system with most, but not all, of the necessary compounds and an inactive set of nanites. If you're sure, you then have 24 hours to take the second pill, which will trigger termination. If you do not, your system will clear the treatment components without side effects. Do you understand?" Panya nodded, holding back tears at the weight of the thing.

Samara leaned over and began removing the sensors from Panya's head and body. She allowed her hand to brush the tears that finally broke free from the girl's face as she detached the devices. Samara might be hard and cynical at times, but Samara was still human and a woman. She counted her lucky stars that she never had to deal with an unwanted pregnancy. Aden had been the only lover she had known, and he had been snipped before the war, a decision he made with his wife after their second child was born. He, at the time, had no idea that his family would be brutally murdered by the Golodoths a year later during his time away in the armed services.

He never bothered to reverse the vasectomy. The way he saw it, he had his chance at procreation and blew it royally. Bringing more children into the world after the ones he loved so dearly had been taken from him was not part of his future. Besides, day-to-day, he never really felt he was going to be around much longer anyway.

The door to the Sick Bay slid open, revealing Takashi with his bloodied right hand loosely wrapped in a rag. "The captain said you better take a look at this," he said, presenting the injured appendage.

Samara unwrapped the crude bandage. "What's this? One of Oliver's rags?" she huffed at him while examining the cuts and abrasions to his hand.

Takashi nodded apologetically.

"Ya' know, don't come crying to me when your hand falls off," Samara said.

Panya rose from the bed and hit a button on the panel that retracted it into the wall as Takashi turned to her. He was undoubtedly sympathetic to the part of her plight he was aware of. Space travel was not for the weak-stomached, and he knew it. "Rough ride, huh?"

Panya mustered a nod. It was rougher than he could imagine.

△△△

The Magellan skimmed above the tops of the tree-like vegetation toward an enormous clearing in the center of a massive forest. Besides Mech, Aden, and Wade were the only ones on the bridge. While Wade went about his business checking the consoles for signs of physical damage and running diagnostics, Aden contemplated the exotic terrain on the monitor before him.

"This place always reminds me of our training camp on Braxus," he said.

"I'm not in the mood for reminiscing," groused Wade, too absorbed in the task at hand.

"Come on, Wade. We used to have so much fun. Remember sneaking out in the woods with the twins after lockdown?" Aden had a broad smile on his face. Those were good times.

Aden and Wade were a lot younger back then. Fresh from school, kids were barely seventeen when they were drafted into the United Organization Task Force during what would ultimately be the end of the 2nd Berillion War. Back then, they were invincible and full of life. Wade was almost easygoing in those days, with no sign of the stick that Aden thought had become permanently stuck up his ass for most of the latter half of his years.

"War is not fun," reminded Wade, raining on Aden's parade.

"At least we felt alive," Aden retorted. "I don't know about you, but since it ended, I feel like I've been living on borrowed time."

As the Magellan entered the clearing, a rectangular metal grid was revealed on the ground. Roughly the size of the ship, the primary port's landing pad had lighted pylons at each corner and flashing lights on the ground around its perimeter. The vessel gently positioned itself over the area and deployed its chunky landing gear. Vented smoke and gases filled the underside as it settled perfectly onto the grid. As the engines' roar subsided, the docking port's flashing lights ceased their rhythmic pulses and switched off.

ΔΔΔ

The stark briefing room of the Magellan held a small table toward the front with a large display on the wall close by. The entire crew sat with their complete attention on the captain as he addressed them. "So far, all onboard sensors or Mech attempts to find human life signs have failed. Considering Prime's history of anomalous dampening fields, this is not unusual, but it certainly looks odd given the situation."

Oliver chimed in. "Have you at least got a scan-lock on the base camp?" This standard procedure was performed by the Mech from outside the ship and was typically done if a comm signal was suddenly lost or degraded due to atmospheric anomalies.

"We're not receiving any signals or return on our ping to their coordinates," Aden informed them. A concerned murmur filled the room.

"How's that possible?" asked Samara.

"It isn't."

To Aden's understanding, the choice was binary — either the base camp was there, and you got a scan lock, or it wasn't, and you didn't. Given that it would be physically impossible for the survey team to up and move, this created a problem: From the perspective of all sensors, the camp was simply not there.

Wade stood up and joined the captain at the front. It was time for the XO to say his piece. "Because a flyover is impossible, sending out a search party makes the most sense."

The room erupted with objections. Oliver's voice rang over the racket. "Do you have brain worms? We don't know this place. Who knows what we'll run into if we go out there? This place is known for what's *unknown* about it. Hell, they can't even tell if half of what lives here is plant or animal life or some weird something else. This is crazy."

The fact that she was a genius wasn't needed for Panya to figure out that stepping off this ship into the strange environment of Vega Prime was not a good idea. "You want us to go *out there*?"

"Captain, you said yourself, we don't even know if base camp still exists," said Takashi, attempting to be the voice of reason.

"What if the wildlife got them?" posed Oliver.

Frustrated, Aden grit his teeth. "Our options are limited here. We're obviously getting no help from the company, and we have to do something."

"It's not our job," exclaimed Oliver. "This is not what we signed up for."

This remark only further agitated Aden. "So, what then? Drop off the supplies and *sayonara*, job well done?!"

"That's not what I mean," Oliver replied defensively.

Samara decided to pipe in before tempers flared any further. "I think what he's saying is we're ill-equipped to help them if they are in trouble."

"We could risk our lives just to be killed ourselves," he added.

Part of Aden agreed with Oliver and Samara, but they didn't really have a choice. There might be lives on the line, and the one thing he had learned and held on to from his years in the service was that you put the lives of others before your own. Otherwise, what was the point of living?

"The closest ship is light-years away. If the survey team is alive and in danger, we're their best and possibly *only* hope," he explained. "We have to do something."

The room settled. As much as the crew wanted to argue the point, the captain was right. The survey team may need their help. What would happen if they didn't get it because the crew of the Magellan was too afraid, too cowardly?

Oliver sighed as Wade again took center stage, now thoroughly irritated. "A search party appears to be the only option," he said with an air of condescension. "We'll take the runabout to base camp and see what we find."

Knowing that he was asking a lot of his crew, Aden tried to calm their fears. "As far as we know, everything could be fine," he offered. "Like O'Neil said, they've been pretty lax on their communications lately."

Samara was the one to ask the question on everyone's mind. "So, who's going to go?"

"Wade's going to head the party, and he'll take Takashi and Mech," Aden replied.

There were more grumblings from the crew. Takashi turned to a relieved Oliver Tross. "That's what I get for knowing how to drive the runabout," he said sarcastically.

In full captain mode, Aden concluded the debate. "This is my decision, so deal with it." He walked briskly to the door as everyone got up from their seats. Samara was pissed, her eyes seethed with anger, and Aden could feel them burning into his back.

ΔΔΔ

The door to Aden's quarters slid open and sharp footsteps followed him through the doorway. He had known Samara would not be pleased with his decision to keep her on the ship before he named the ground team. The rest was inevitable.

"Do I look like a child to you?" she spat out at him the instant the door closed behind them. "If they need medical attention, I'm the only one qualified."

"I'm not getting into this with you," he informed her calmly.

Samara grabbed his bicep. "What the fuck Aden? What the *actual fuck?*" she snarled. "I don't need you to protect me."

Aden didn't raise his voice in return. "Are you sure about that?" he asked her. This discussion was beginning to sound more like a parent and a child than one between two equals.

"You know damn well I am," she hissed back.

Aden studied the face of his young companion. This was not about going on a rescue mission but challenging his orders. Like a child testing the boundaries of a parent, Samara had grown more and more predictable in her rebellious behavior. Lately, it had become more of an issue; right now, that issue ran the risk of getting her killed.

Their passion had long been displaced by slowly increasing resentment and avoidance. Aden didn't blame her for her part. He was surprised it took her this long to rebel. It wasn't that she didn't love him; her love and loyalty to him were the roots of all their problems. It sometimes confused the hell out of their working relationship, and this was one of the worst times it had happened so far.

He looked at her soft young hand, holding fast to the

weathered fabric of his flight jacket. *"Let go of me,"* he implored her.

There was a sad moment. She knew what he really meant but now was not the time. She slowly released her hold on him as her hand slumped to her side, then turned and exited his quarters without another word.

CHAPTER FIVE

The rear bay door of the Magellan slowly opened, and a ramp extended to the surface of the landing pad. The runabout, a big beast that looked part truck and part tank, sat in the middle of the hangar located in the rear of the ship. It was mostly enclosed, with portals on its side and a large hatch on top. The windshield was made of aluminum-reinforced glass and covered by a titanium grille for good measure. A gun turret was mounted toward the front of the roof just behind where the two front seats were in the cab near the roof hatch. The rear of the roof carried various forms of scanning equipment, and there were lights mounted around the periphery just below the roof line. As Oliver and Mech checked out the vehicle, its six massive tires making them look small, Takashi and Panya hauled in another crate.

Having been a great proponent of education (forced or not) for his whole life, Takashi had taken it upon himself to teach Panya a thing or two about Vega Prime. "Prime has a bunch of areas that are...um... no-fly zones," he was saying.

"But this is an emergency. Couldn't they make an exception?" asked Panya, confused why these rules would supersede the safety of the people they're designed to supposedly protect on the ground.

"It's not a rule, actually," informed Takashi. "There are atmospheric and magnetic distortions over big areas that mess with guidance controls and flight systems. They lost a *lot* of ships figuring that out." That was an understatement.

In the first six months of the first exploration of Vega Prime by the United Organization, over 20 manned and then later 200 unmanned vessels were deployed around the surface to map out these inexplicably random "no-fly zones." Not one of them returned. The wreckage of most hadn't even been found. It was as if Prime ate them.

This was maddening to the scientific community because the locations of the dampening fields were so utterly random, *and* they seemed to move in some fashion. They had determined they were not caused by any natural anomalies on the ground or controlled by pressures from the upper or lower atmosphere. Scientists spent months assessing the phenomena from space to see if some form of radiation was causing the issues, but the lack of any consistent data just made them even more frustrated. In all the studies of Vega Prime, one thing remained true: the data didn't make any sense.

To this day, only a tenth of the planet's no fly-zones was definitively known, and the crew of the Magellan had learned to avoid coming even a hundred miles from the closest ones when making their deliveries. The ones that were unknown were even more dangerous, and the risk of encountering them if a flight wasn't perfectly plotted was very high.

After learning all this from Takashi, something didn't add up for Panya. "Then why would the survey team build their base camp under one of those areas?"

"Probably the same reason they would travel light years to live on a screwed-up planet inhabited by monsters," Takashi offered as he flared his eyes and twirled his finger around his ear like a madman. He was grinning.

"Aren't you afraid?" she asked. A hint of fear hid under her voice as she asked.

"Yeah…" he began before being harshly interrupted by the XO on his way by.

Wade stood above them on the roof of the vehicle, looking down on them like a tyrant. "Would you two stop dawdling and get her loaded up!" He barked. The pair went back to work quietly, and Panya thought about what they might be getting themselves into.

△△△

Wade and Takashi stood by the runabout, now parked outside the ship. Dressed for the elements, Wade double-checked their gear on a tablet as Mech stowed the remaining food rations. Samara suddenly emerged from the ship dressed for travel and carrying a large duffel. Wade eyed her curiously as she approached. "I think we've got everything...."

Ignoring the comment altogether, she walked right by him, opened the back hatch of the runabout, and hurled her bag inside. He watched as she swung open the cockpit door and jumped in the passenger seat. "Now you've got everything," she corrected him in a nonchalant tone of voice.

Furiously, Wade slammed down the tablet and leaned into the cockpit opening. "This is my ground team. I give the orders here!"

Samara threw a look at his scarred hand on the door frame. The burns were old, but they were still fresh wounds as far as some of the crew were concerned. "Yeah. We all know what happens when you give the orders." She looked into his eyes. Wade's face blossomed bright red. He looked like he was going to explode with rage.

"She's joining the ground team," came a voice from behind. Wade spun around to see Aden exiting the ship with Oliver at his side. "You'll need her in case of any medical emergencies."

"I think I can more than handle that," Wade retorted. "I have years of medical training."

"I know. But what if something happens to *you*?" He added firmly, "I'm not taking any chances. Understood?"

Samara locked eyes with Aden and gave him an unemotional nod. Her eyes went back to Wade and tightened. She had the upper hand, and she decided to push it. "Are you going to shut the door? It's getting chilly in here."

Too furious to go head-to-head with Samara in front of Aden, he snatched up the tablet and stormed over to Takashi and Mech. "Load in. It's not going to be light out all day!" This was classic displacement, and Samara enjoyed seeing it in action. What was the point of having Wade around if you couldn't ruffle his feathers every now and again? As far as she was concerned, he had more than earned her spite. The man was a prick.

Now completely loaded up, Wade, Takashi, and Mech headed into the runabout. All business, Aden turned to the remaining crew members. "I want a full inspection of the hull," he ordered Oliver. "Let's see what damage those drifters caused." He then turned to Panya. "You can help me inventory our supplies. Let's assume we're going to have some visitors...."

The roar of the runabout's engines firing up drowned him out before he could finish. They turned to watch the vehicle drive off and disappear into the jungle. Deep down, Aden was worried for Samara and the team. Call it caution, call it paranoia — it was there nonetheless, and as they turned back to the task at hand he couldn't shake the feeling.

ΔΔΔ

The transport rolled through the dense foliage knocking down the alien plant life in a wide swath as it rumbled on.

Its six massive tires cut a path almost eight feet wide through the landscape, leaving a scar on the land in its wake. Slightly obscured by tree-like growths, the sun still shone brightly in the sky.

Takashi sat in the driver's seat, maintaining their course with an air of confidence. Next to him, Samara stared off into the distance. She felt a pang of regret about how she had been treating Aden. She knew she was bottling up her genuine emotions and that when they managed to bubble to the surface they became hostility. When she was in the middle of one of their fights, she felt helpless to take a step back and see what she was doing. Her part in it. Aden had always been good to her. Always. And it seemed the only way she knew how to repay it lately was with disdain for him. How it had come to this over time, she had a grasp of. She had grown up, pure and simple, as Aden had grown older. The seasons of their lives were out of sync with their affection for each other.

How to make it stop was an entirely different animal. The real question now was which one of them was finally going to put an end to it. At the moment, it was still anyone's game. She wiped a single tear from her eye lest one of the others, especially Wade, catch her with her emotions unguarded. The topic of Aden and their relationship was a mess in her mind, and she had no reason to share it.

Wade and Mech monitored a set of display screens on the wall of the rear section of the interior compartment. The runabout had ample space for at least four or five extra passengers, hopefully more if necessary. The android spouted out some navigational corrections. Takashi adjusted his course as Wade looked on.

"Thanks, Meg," acknowledged Takashi.

Wade looked at Takashi, having picked up on the new nickname. "Why did you call it that?"

"Excuse me, Sir?"

"You heard me. Its name is 'Mech' or 'Alpha 5-430'," reminded Wade, referring to the android's make and model number.

Samara chimed in. "Didn't you hear? Mech is Takashi's new girlfriend."

Red appeared on Takashi's cheeks. "I've just made some minor mods, that's all. Nothing that would void the warranty."

Wade still didn't like it. "I've already spoken with you about messing with it. The thing is twitchy enough as it is."

"That's not true. Ever since I made those adjustments to Meg's...Mech's decision core, it's been working fine. I know you noticed," he added with conviction.

"I still don't think it's wise. Especially with you acting like it's a person."

"I think you're making a big deal out of nothing, Wade," Takashi retorted. "What's the problem if I try to give her some personality?" He then added to Samara's amazement, "Lord knows if it's one thing missing from this crew, it's *that*."

Samara was rather impressed with the young man. That took some balls that she had previously thought he just didn't have. Mech was more important to him than she thought too, which made it a little harder for her to poke fun at him.

Wade shook his head. It was, he thought, his lot in life to suffer such fools. He turned back to the robot. "How soon, Mech?" Mech's response made Wade even more irritated. "Unable to process request."

"Meg, how soon until we arrive at the previously specified coordinates?" repeated Takashi, trying to diffuse the situation.

"At current velocity, 11.37 minutes," answered the machine.

All this earned more venom from Wade. "If you're going to spend time messing with Mech, why don't you fix *that*?"

"It's not that big a deal," he said. "She understands well enough if you speak clearly."

"It's a pain in the ass," he said, then turned to Samara for support. "Don't you agree?"

Samara did agree but was having more fun watching this amusing little farce. "Personally, Wade, I don't get worked up over things like that." She turned back around in her seat and ignored him.

"That's right." Wade chuffed at her. "It's everything else you get worked up about."

Before she had a chance to respond, Takashi intervened with some more pertinent information. "I think we're entering a clearing."

All eyes turned and looked out of the front windshield.

ΔΔΔ

Back on board the Magellan, Aden rifled through some storage cabinets located in the rear of the command center. He retrieved something stashed behind some boxes stuffed into a cabinet as Panya entered. She looked troubled. "Sir, the supplies...It's going to get awfully slim before we get back to the far colony," she informed him. "If this turns into a rescue, it's going to get *really* tight."

"We'll be fine," he replied confidently. He held out a small handheld device to her. "Would you give this to Oliver? He was looking for it." Taking it from him, she headed for the door, but Aden stopped her before she got more than a couple of feet. "Hey, Panya. I am sorry about teasing you before about being a whiz at the comm," he apologized with all sincerity. "That was my specialty back in the day." He continued. "Nowhere near your grades, though."

Panya forced an awkward smile and then exited. As she traveled through the main corridor toward the rear airlock, she reflected on what the captain had said to her and wished she had the confidence to act with more decisiveness. She tried to convince herself that this kind of conviction comes with age and experience, but she knew that was bullshit. There were plenty of people her age that had self-confidence and ambition in spades, so if she truly was going to make something of herself, she needed to get her shit together and toughen up. What kind of example would she be to a growing child? As her brain fretted over that new tangent, it once again dredged up her fears and insecurities about her pregnancy.

Opening the main airlock hatch, she stepped outside and walked down the short ramp to the surface. As she traced her way along the exterior hull, she saw Oliver up ahead, working on the front landing gear. Since she was focused on him, she didn't notice the piles of tools littered on the ground. Her foot caught a large wrench, and she fell down face-first onto the rubberized landing pad. As she hit the ground, the device she'd been carrying slipped from her hand and bounced out of her reach.

"Idiot," she chastised herself. Wincing in pain, she crawled forward to retrieve the lost item. As she reached for it, something small entered her line of vision and slowly approached.

A bipedal creature about the size of a guinea pig sauntered toward her. Its near-translucent yellowish body was smooth and hairless, and it had two small appendages that ended in what looked like little three-fingered hands. The body shape was bulbous, with gill-like slits running up the front. It had tiny, stumpy legs and big feet that pattered along on the pad. It made strange noises as it moved.

Panya froze as it came closer. She could feel all the hair on her body stand at attention as a chill surged through her. Was this how it all ended?

Stopping a mere foot from her hand, the creature rested on its little legs and produced a high-pitched chattering sound. This broke Panya from her trance, and she quickly scrambled back as her fear response kicked in. The tiny organism perked up in reaction to the sudden movement and stumbled toward her. Panicking, she raced backward on the ground until she smacked her head against the hull of the ship full force -- the blow nearly knocking her back down. The creature jumped on the dazed girl's legs and climbed up her body, stopping just below her breasts and on top of her belly. There it nestled into her clothes, pawing at them with both arms. It made small murmuring sounds. Its body pulsed.

A moment later, a large shadow appeared over her. "What the hell is *that?!*" It was Oliver. He stood over the dazed and frightened girl, looking down at the thing attached to her clothes.

Panya had no idea what to do. "Get it off me!"

He grabbed its body, but the texture was like a jellyfish, making it hard for Oliver to get a firm hold. "Come on, you mother— "

Suddenly, the creature emitted a piercing howl that erupted in Oliver's head, filling his mind. It was a searing sensation that only he was experiencing. In his hands the creature's body hardened, its skin becoming more rigid and more textured. Panya watched Oliver start to writhe around, confused at what he was doing. He suddenly released the creature and reached for his ears. By the time they got there, the sound filling his head had ceased.

"Help me!" Begged Panya. It was quivering and making small chattering noises. Panya realized that it didn't have anything even like a face — the sound was coming from its small gill slits. She was horrified.

Reaching into his back pocket, Oliver produced a lock-back utility knife. He grabbed hold of Panya's blouse, stretching it from her body. Jabbing the blade through the material, he sliced a chunk of her shirt off and hurled it away, creature and all. "Are you alright?" he asked as he leaned over her. As he examined her now exposed midriff for marks, he noticed her slightly distended belly.

Nervously, her eyes searched his: *Does he realize I'm pregnant?* Before Oliver could comment, Aden burst out of the ship. "What's going on?!"

Helping Panya to her feet, Oliver quickly took off his jacket and covered her up. He pointed to the critter perched in the middle of the discarded piece of her shirt. "That thing attacked Panya."

Aden followed his finger to the tiny creature flailing about in the pile of fabric. "We better check it out then," instructed the captain as he placed a fatherly hand on Panya's shoulder. "Let's get you inside." Her face went flush as her emotions overtook her. Whether it was the unexpected scare or the hormones currently wreaking havoc on her body, she grabbed onto Aden and let it all out.

ΔΔΔ

Seen through the windshield, the exotic vegetation began to thin out as the runabout entered the clearing. Samara scanned the immediate area. This did not look good. "We should see it by now."

Wade had his own opinion. "You got us lost, Takashi," he said accusingly.

"These are the coordinates," he replied, exasperated.

"If you're right, then where's the base camp? We should see it by now."

The runabout came to a sudden stop as everyone lurched

in their seats. Without a word, Takashi unbuckled his seatbelt, got up, and bolted from the vehicle. Confusion crossed over the faces of Wade and Samara.

"Where the hell are you going?!" barked Wade. It didn't make a difference -- Takashi was out of earshot within seconds. Left without any other choice, Wade and Samara followed.

"Takashi, wait!" called out Samara as they climbed out and tried to catch up to him. Ahead of them, Takashi suddenly slowed and came to a stop at the crest of an incline piled high with dirt and weird-looking debris. As the others joined him, they immediately saw what he was racing to. It was the edge of a cliff that looked into an enormous trench below. A large crevice lay below them, nearly a hundred feet deep and more than three times as wide. It was as if the ground had been ripped away and removed in one motion by a giant earthmover or the hand of a god.

Takashi could barely speak. "This isn't *possible*."

The survey team's base camp was gone.

"We're in the wrong place," Wade repeated adamantly.

"No. This is the right place," corrected Takashi. "I'm *sure* of it."

CHAPTER SIX

Wade's face was on the main viewscreen in the Magellan's bridge as Aden tried to absorb and process the new information. "Gone? How can it be *gone*?"

"We don't know, sir," was all Wade could offer at the moment. This was certainly perplexing.

"Could the crater be from an asteroid?" asked the captain.

"Mech searched the area. There's no sign of any impact," came Wade's reply. "It looks like the whole area was just... removed."

Out of breath, Takashi came into view behind Wade on the screen. "Meg's got a life sign... It's human."

"Captain?" Wade looked back at Aden.

The answer was already evident to all three of them. "Go check it out," Aden said.

∆∆∆

The runabout barreled into the clearing, staying close to the rim of the cliff and circling its way down along it so as to avoid flipping over. It bucked up and down as it rolled over the increasingly rocky terrain. The crew held on tight as they got thrown left and right. Samara and Wade monitored the scanners and other instruments, searching for any more information while Takashi drove. Not much was forthcoming.

"Take it easy, Takashi," yelled Wade over the engines. "There's no point to this if we kill ourselves before we get there." Takashi just ignored him. There were lives on the line, and every second might count. He had learned from Aden long ago that some principles are more important than yourself, and the preservation of life was one of them. If even one of the scientists could be saved, they had to do it. If, in doing so, they found more, it would be doubly worth it. Takashi was resolved.

In the back, Mech monitored its internal bio-tracker and supplied real-time course corrections. It was jacked into the vehicle and spoke through all of its internal speakers at once. "Adjust West 7°." A beeping sensor buried within Mech pulsed faster as they closed in on their mark. "Target interception in 4.75 minutes."

Samara pointed to a small hill below them and off to the left, partially obscured by a small ridge of dirt and debris. "It's got to be over there."

Takashi leaned on the pedal and cut left as the truck careened and bounced over to the small hill. He suddenly slammed on the brakes, and the runabout came to a screeching halt at its peak, fishtailing as it did so. A sizeable open expanse lay before them on the other side of the hill, thickly inhabited by a herd of bizarre-looking animals. Like a cross between a rhinoceros and a cow, they had coarse humped backs covered in stringy braids of hair-like tentacles that loosely swayed and slapped against the beast's leathery brown hide. What appeared to be the heads of the creatures were adorned with a geometric pattern of spikes and horns. About forty of them stood apart from each other and took no notice of the arrival of the runabout.

Samara exited the truck with a pair of image-enhancing binoculars. She held them up to her eyes and scanned the area, flipping on their augmented reality info display. She saw crystal clear images laced with annotations through them — most of which were woefully incomplete or otherwise useless. Prime was still mainly a mystery. One notation, connected by a small line to the nearest beast in her field of view, said "Paraxion." Some of the animals had been cataloged, which was good. She continued to scan the herd until he froze on one of the animals.

Attached to its side was what appeared to be a human being. The man, dressed in a tattered blue jumpsuit, was pressed against the paraxion's midsection and held in place by a mass of tentacles. His face was obscured by a membrane that stretched between them and covered most of his head and neck.

As the rest of the crew exited the truck, Takashi noticed the grave expression on Samara's face. "What is it?"

"Take a look." Samara tagged the beast with the binoculars positioning system, then handed them to him and pointed to the paraxion far off in the distance.

He looked through the binoculars and saw exactly what she wanted him to. "Jesus Christ!"

Wade snatched the glasses from Takashi and looked for himself. He snapped to a decision in seconds and handed the binoculars back to Samara. "Send in Mech to retrieve him."

"Are you *crazy*?!" blurted out Takashi, "What if they hurt her?" It was a knee-jerk reaction, and he regretted saying it the second it left his mouth. Especially his use of the word "her" in front of Wade.

"It's a fucking robot!" Wade replied incredulously. "By all means, Takashi, feel free to go in its place." Wade wasn't finished with the young tech officer. "This is exactly why I don't want you messing with the Mech and giving it human attributes. It confuses things. When we get back to the Magellan, I want you to change its voice back. Do you understand me?" Biting his lip, Takashi nodded to his superior officer. "And if you give me any more crap or disregard another of my orders, you'll be off the Magellan so fast you won't know what hit you."

"I think he gets it, Wade," interjected Samara. "Can we get back to business?"

Wade gestured at the Mech, "Well? Get to it."

Completely humiliated, Takashi crossed to the droid. It took all his strength to swallow his pride and stay focused after one of Wade's dressing-downs. "Meg," his voice wavered, "we need you to approach the human forward of our position and determine his condition." He then made some adjustments to the robot'. "I will relay new instructions when you are in position. Understood?"

"Affirmative." came the reply.

Mech's mellifluous female voice calmed him slightly. He gently pat the robot's arm and whispered to it. "Be careful."

Undaunted, Mech sauntered by the three of them on a direct path toward the creatures in the field. Oblivious to any danger, the robot entered the herd, walking within mere inches of touching them.

Remarkably, the paraxions took no interest in the invader. Mech continued its robotic stroll toward its destination. It walked right up to the one with the human hostage and immediately extended its arm to perform its instructed task. Mech's hand unfolded, exposing a small array of sensors that it held in front of the stomach of the man. Its hand gently swept up and down his torso gathering information. The task proceeded without incident from the man or the beast.

Takashi watched the action through the binoculars as Mech relayed the information over the team's comms. "Human male approximate age thirty-four years is comatose due to an unidentified neurotoxin in his bloodstream."

"Await further instructions." Takashi threw a look at Wade and Samara.

Samara was the first to speak. "They didn't seem to notice Mech was even there," she observed. "Do you think it's safe?"

Wade considered the possibilities as his eyes wandered from the herd of paraxions to the vehicle behind him. "They're too tightly packed to get the runabout any closer." He turned back to Takashi. "Get Mech to try and move it away from the rest." He requested calmly.

Takashi took a deep breath. This was what he was afraid of. "Meg, try to move the organism away from the herd. Determine optimal course and execute."

The robot repositioned itself at the rear of the paraxion and extended both arms. Planting its feet into the ground, it clamped into the harsh soil below to get maximum leverage. It gently shoved the animal.

Nothing happened. The beast didn't react, nor did it budge.

Takashi's voice sounded over the monitor speaker of the Mech's internal comm. "Increase pressure."

Mech's mechanics squealed as it pushed the animal harder. Remarkably, Mech's feet began to slide backward, their secondary clamps cutting trenches into the soil.

Wade shook his head in amazement as he dropped his pair of binoculars. "How much does that thing weigh?" The animal weighed more than would logically make sense. A Model 5 Mechanoid could easily push the runabout, yet this one couldn't get this beast to even budge an inch. "Alright. That's enough." He said.

"You can stop, Meg." Ordered Takashi.

Mech immediately retracted its appendages and stood at attention by the paraxion, awaiting the next request.

Wade nodded his head as he addressed the ground team. "Let's go in for a better look."

Takashi panicked. "I'm not going in there."

"I wasn't talking to you." Wade snapped back at the young

man. "I need you to stay by the runabout in case this goes south."

Samara retrieved two hand-held particle blasters from the truck and handed one to Wade. "Well. This is shaping up to be quite a day."

ΔΔΔ

On a table in the middle of the Magellan's science lab rested a nearly seamless cube of aluminum-reinforced glass. Inside the cell, the tiny creature, still holding onto a fabric scrap, randomly waved one of its arms around and extended its fingers. Oliver busied himself with some data from the most recent bio-scans on it as Panya entered. Pulling up a nearby chair, she seated herself by the cube and peered in on the organism. Curiously she watched the tiny arm flail about as Oliver crossed over to her. "It's been doing that for over ten minutes now."

Panya was mesmerized by its movement. "Do you think it was trying to hurt me?" she asked. "I mean, maybe it was just being friendly."

"I don't know," Oliver shrugged. "I did some preliminary scans and it appears to be... safe. At least, as far as I know, anyway. The database identified it as something called an "Altricion," but I'll be darned if I know what the hell that is. It didn't seem to mind that I touched it this time, though." He added, with an air of self-deprecation, "I'm no scientist. I wish Takashi were here." Picking up a tablet from the table, he headed for the door. "I've got to get back to the bridge."

Panya's eyes were intensely focused on the altricion. "I'm going to stay here for a bit."

This concerned Oliver just slightly. He didn't know if it was wise for her to be alone with the organism. He wasn't worried that it would hurt her; he just didn't know Panya well enough yet to completely understand her motivations. Unfortunately, he had work to do elsewhere on the ship -- those nav consoles wouldn't fix themselves. He exited the science lab leaving her to her own devices.

Panya continued to study the creature, watching its moving appendage stop and then extend at her. Sitting up, the alien stumbled forward, halting only when it hit the wall of the chamber.

Intrigued, she leaned in closer as the altricion pressed all its fingers against the transparent wall. Poor thing, she thought. It looked so helpless. It reminded her of a newborn kitten finding its way in the strange environment outside its mother's womb. Slowly, she reached toward the top of the cube. As her hand traveled upwards, the creature's arm-like appendages followed until they were raised high above. Panya couldn't help herself; she needed to touch it even though, intellectually, she understood the potential risk. *"Panya, look with your eyes, not with your hands,"* her parents used to scold. They were cold people, doling out hugs and kisses only in rare instances. Panya was more "touchy-feely," as she referred to it.

Unlatching the lock, Panya lifted the lid and slowly slid in her hand. The altricion continued to reach skyward for her as her bare hand closed the small distance. Suddenly, both tiny hands gently grasped around her fingers. Her first instinct was to withdraw, but as she tensed the fingers let go of her hand.

Panya studied her hand, now free of the cage. There was nothing wrong with it. No burns or bruises, no tingling feelings. Her empirical assessment suggested that this tiny creature had no evil or clandestine intentions. "You're not gonna hurt me, are you?" She whispered to the little critter. Once again, lowering her hand into the cell, she touched the gelatinous flesh of the organism. It responded by reaching for her and wrapping its fingers around her wrist. Panya smiled lovingly.

△△△

Takashi watched through his binoculars as Wade and Samara entered the herd. Sweat trickled down his forehead in anticipation. You wouldn't catch him doing something this foolhardy; they had no idea what these creatures were capable of. In the blink of an eye, Takashi could not only have a lonely ride back to the Magellan and have to explain how their XO and Medical Officer were eaten by these supposedly "docile" monsters. This was bad news. He just knew it.

Weapons drawn, Samara and Wade slowly approached the first of the massive beasts. The hump on its back towered over them, and as they entered the pack, they quickly became lost in the sea of monsters. Surprisingly Samara was not the least bit concerned. It was such a surreal experience that her brain seemed to disconnect and let her feel like this wasn't really happening or that she would undoubtedly get a do-over if anything *did* happen. Wade, on the other hand, had lived life long enough to know when he was putting himself in harm's way. He had a job to do, and as long as he stayed focused on the task at hand, he'd make it through this no matter what happened. Wade had been in worse situations and made it through to the other side. Even though one of them had left him scarred both physically and emotionally, he had not given up on the value of *seeing things through*. It was the difference between him and those he thought less of in this job, and he was unable to let it go.

Fortunately, they passed through the herd without incident. As they approached their target they were greeted by Mech. "Awaiting new instructions."

"Mech, stand back so we can get a look." requested Samara.

As the robot took a stride away from the paraxion, Samara

and Wade moved in next to it, eyes transfixed on the man glued to its side. Both their eyes scanned the patch on his tattered jumpsuit identifying him as one V. REED.

"He's from the survey team," Wade surmised.

"Obviously," Samara dug at him.

"Give it a rest, Samara." This wasn't the time or place for her sarcasm. He tightly grasped the handle of the pistol in his right hand as he moved closer to the docile creature. "Alright. I'm going to touch it." As he extended his left hand, Samara took a defensive posture, firmly gripping her weapon in both hands.

"Ready whenever you are," Samara informed him.

Cautiously, Wade touched the side of the creature. The skin felt leathery but compressed under his touch, almost like a gel.

Nothing happened.

He gave it a shove... Nothing.

"Apparently, this thing could give a shit about *us*," he postulated. Without another word, they both grabbed the tentacles connecting it to V. REED and tried to pry the man loose. They were as strong as steel cables and equally unmovable as they stiffened against their attempts to release them. The creature was not letting go. They backed away in frustration.

"Now what?" asked Samara. She certainly wasn't ready to admit defeat.

Wade strode to the front of the beast and aimed his gun at the side of the thing's head. "Plan B."

Samara's eyes went wide. Not in her wildest imagination did she envision Wade doing something as reckless as he was about to do. "No!" she cried -- but it was far too late.

The pistol discharged a blast into the paraxion from point blank range, disintegrating the body part into mist and flying chunks. The beast howled in enormous pain as it reared up --

but not in the direction Wade had assumed it would. What he thought was the tail end rose high above him as a mouth-like orifice billowed open and hissed at him. This was followed by an equally horrific cry from the entire herd. Samara tackled Wade to the ground and rolled away as the paraxion slammed the front two of its feet into the soil, exactly where he was standing mere seconds before. The man attached to its side flopped around like a rag doll, unresponsive.

"You *asshole!*" Samara screamed at him. "That was its tail!"

Samara and Wade scrambled to their feet as the paraxion took off with the entire herd in tow. Samara, Wade, and Mech were suddenly in the center of a growing stampede.

Samara grabbed the robot by the arm. "Mech, back to the runabout!" Wade grabbed the other arm and held on, both using the mechanoid as a sort of anchor against the press of the oncoming herd. The three of them methodically cut through the herd, trying to avoid the panicking monsters that raced by them. It was slow going.

Takashi watched the chaos unfold from the safety of the hill above. A moment later, his comm erupted.

"Takashi! Takashi! Rev up the runabout!" Samara screamed in his ear over the din of the rampaging paraxions.

Racing into the vehicle, he started up the engines and floored the accelerator as he turned toward the ground crew in the valley below. He could barely make out Samara and the others as they weaved through the chaos. It was a miracle that none of them had been trampled by the big beasts. As he sped closer, he got the bright idea of activating the distress siren. With the flick of a switch, the external speakers on the runabout screeched with the high pitch wail of its warning horns. The effect was immediate. The paraxions began to break apart and run in random directions, scattering everywhere to escape the irritating sound coming from the big metal animal that had come into the clearing. Fortunately, this opened a path directly to the crew for the runabout. Leaning on the accelerator, he made a straight run for them, closing the distance in no time and skidding to a stop. He hit the side hatch release on his console as he pulled up. Samara, Wade, and Mech safely jumped inside as Takashi flicked off the distress siren. He gave his mates an accusatory look. "What did you do?!"

Samara was breathing so hard she couldn't talk as Wade laughed between gulps of air. She jabbed her hand in the direction of the charging creatures and strained to speak. "Follow...the...wounded...one..." She coughed. "Don't lose him!"

As Takashi shook his head and slammed on the pedal, Wade finally caught his breath. "It feels like the old days again."

"You could have gotten us killed!" Samara yelled at him.

"What happened out there?" asked Takashi. "I saw a blast right before the stampede."

Samara pointed an accusatory finger at the XO. "This idiot shot the thing in the ass."

In an atypical moment for Wade, he stifled a laugh instead of getting high and mighty. "I thought it was its head. It was an honest mistake." He was snickering.

When the siren ceased, the paraxions began to form back up into a marauding herd headed toward the horizon. It took Takashi racing at top speed to catch up and overtake them. The runabout entered the charging pack from the rear. As it barreled through, the paraxions were forced to break off from the main group in different directions. Takashi could make out the wounded one with a man dangling from its side directly ahead. "I've got him." He informed the others.

"We need to separate him from the pack. Can you do that?" Wade asked.

"I'll do my best, but then what?"

"I've got an idea." He gave Takashi a pat on the shoulder

and smiled for once before disappearing into the rear of the runabout. For the first time, Takashi was beginning to see a different side of Wade and that maybe he wasn't such an ass after all. A smirk of confidence lit up his face.

Amused by his reaction, Samara chuckled. "What, are you two buddies now?" she joked.

"Jealous?" he retorted. His spirits were high, and Takashi was focused on the task at hand. He was going to catch that rogue creature if it was the last thing he did. Luckily the beast was starting to slow down as it headed toward a rocky hill flanked by some tall outgrowths. The young pilot maneuvered the runabout to the paraxion's left side and gave a quick burst of the distress siren. The beast flinched and miraculously raced in the exact direction Takashi wanted. As it continued onward, he slammed on the brakes and cut the wheel. Another quick burst of the irritating sound caused the entire remaining herd coming their way to scatter. Once again slamming on the gas, Takashi returned to his pursuit of the wounded one, now isolated from the pack. "Alright, Wade. She's all yours". He yelled to the rear of the runabout.

"Good work, Takashi," replied Wade. Opening a hatch above him, the XO slipped upwards to the roof of the runabout. The combination of the wind and the erratic movements of the truck caused him to pitch around wildly. Fighting it, he took control of the mounted cannon and powered it up. As it hummed to life, he scanned the horizon. The rocky alcove looked like the best bet. "Keep it headed toward the rocks," he said to Takashi through the comm. "We can trap it there."

Takashi held the course, keeping the creature directly in front of the runabout as they both began to slow. Coming to a complete stop as it hit the dead end, the paraxion turned to face its pursuer.

"Stop the truck, Takashi," Wade said. "But keep it running."

The wounded beast swayed back and forth as its feet rhythmically beat on the ground. The tentacles on its hide flapped around, including the ones holding onto its human captive. The paraxion then let loose a mighty howl into the sky.

The noise was nearly deafening to Wade. Having had enough, he gripped the handles of the cannon and positioned it for a kill shot. "Now hold still, you ugly--"

Out of nowhere, a huge spear-like appendage shot down from above and skewered the paraxion all the way through.

Reeling back, Wade looked up to see an enormous creature tucked between the rocks of the alcove. This massive crab-like monster's leathery hide mimicked the color and texture of the surrounding rocks almost perfectly, blending it in with the environment. One of its two sword-like hands pierced the paraxion and ran through it into the ground, missing the human hostage by only a few inches. Samara and Takashi couldn't believe their eyes. They had heard of the enormous creature called a Mimesis in stories of Prime, but they had never dreamed of a beast like this, even in their wildest nightmares. They watched, frozen in silence, as the situation unfolded before them.

Just as the creature raised its other limb to deliver the death blow, Wade trained the cannon on it and fired. The limb split off and dropped to the floor in a foul-smelling mess of goo and carapace. Another shot from the cannon caused the sword embedded in the paraxion's midsection to break off near its body. The mimesis retracted what was left of its limbs. With its arms now tucked in and mouth closed, the creature's skin suddenly appeared to transform from leathery hide into a hard protective shell-like covering. To the untrained eye, the creature looked like just another large rock formation.

Wade yelled via his comm to his stunned colleagues. "Use the winch!"

"Takashi, Samara. Do you hear me?!" He came again. "Use

the winch!"

It was Samara who broke from her daze first. As her eyes searched the controls of the runabout, she found what she was looking for: The winch. Depressing a button released a joystick from its casing and she at once took hold of it as a targeting screen appeared on the windshield in front of her. Lining it up on the dying paraxion's body, she made sure to choose a spot as far away from the Man as possible. She pressed the fire button. Moments later, a bolt attached to a tether fired at the beast on the ground. It tore into the creature's flesh and grappled onto its back. The tether immediately tightened.

"Now get us out of here," ordered Wade before jumping down inside the rear cabin.

Slowly, the runabout reversed and dragged the paraxion away from the alcove. The beast's weight put a lot of strain on the engines, and it was slow going to pull it into the nearby clearing. A trail of dark bodily liquid smeared the ground behind it.

Now at a safe distance, the runabout powered down and the crew jumped out. The four of them stood for a moment by the truck as they checked their weapons. This thing could still be dangerous, and after all that, they weren't taking any chances. They cautiously made their way closer to the paraxion.

Samara pointed her weapon at what was now presumed to be the head. "Let's make sure it's out of its misery."

"What if its ...brain isn't in the head?" asked Takashi, afraid of being this close to it.

"That's a good point." Samara fired a round into the head and then randomly blasted the paraxion along its massive frame, being careful to avoid the man. Suddenly, the tentacles went limp, and the man slid off the body into a heap on the ground. Holstering her weapon, Samara reached for him. "Help me," she instructed Takashi. With his aid, they dragged the man away from the beast to a spot near the runabout. Samara pulled the remains of the gooey membrane away from the man's face and checked for a pulse. "He's alive."

ΔΔΔ

The door to the Magellan's science lab slid open, and Aden and Oliver entered in the midst of a conversation. They stopped short at the entrance. Panya sat cross-legged on the floor with the altricion before her, wobbling around at her feet. With a wide grin on her face, she looked up at them. "We're playing," she announced innocently.

They approached her cautiously. "I don't think that's wise," said the captain making sure to keep his voice a metered tone. The last thing he wanted to do was agitate a creature they didn't understand, so he kept his anger in check.

As they came closer, she scooped up the little creature and held it against her breast protectively. "She's not doing anything," Panya said defensively.

"We don't know that," Aden retorted. "We don't know anything about that creature. It could be harming you in ways that you have no understanding of — chemical, radiological, who knows?" As Aden continued to move toward her, Oliver crossed to the transparent case and opened the top. "Why don't you give it to me, and we'll put it back in the containment cube?" suggested Aden.

"No," responded Panya defiantly. She stood up and backed away, clutching the tiny organism closer. "She was frightened in there."

"Panya, listen to the captain," implored Oliver.

She shook her head. "It's wrong to keep her locked up. I won't let you put her back in there."

Aden stopped his advance. "You're being unreasonable." then he added, "and insubordinate."

"No, I'm not. She hasn't tried to hurt me. She's just curious," Panya insisted. "We should just let her go."

Aden was about to burst. He had put up with all types of shenanigans from his crew over the years, but this situation was undoubtedly taking the cake. Either this girl was trying to push his buttons, or she was utterly bonkers. Either way, he wanted it to stop now. "Fine," he barked sternly. "Get it off my ship!"

"I will," she replied. Holding the altricion tenderly in her arms, she swept by the captain and exited the lab.

Aden shook his head and turned to Oliver. "I can't figure that girl out. She's almost as stubborn as Samara sometimes."

"Maternal instinct," answered the Engineer.

"What?"

Oliver looked at him knowingly.

"You've got to be *kidding* me."

How she managed to keep it off her medical evaluation was anyone's guess. Now Aden was really pissed. This meant that she flat-out lied when he interviewed her. Before Aden could continue down this mental rabbit hole, a burst of static emitted from his personal comm.

"Ground team to Magellan. Do you copy?" It was Wade.

Aden spoke into his communicator. "Harker here."

"Captain," Wade began solemnly. "You better sit down for this."

All the captain could think at this point was: *now what?*

CHAPTER SEVEN

Blackness… His eyes fluttered open, letting in the light as blurry faces came into focus. He could hear a distant female voice. "I think he's coming to," she said, then added gently, "Can you hear me, Dr. Reed?" That was his name. Dr. Virgil Reed, exobiologist, Vega Prime survey team member. He could remember this.

Samara and Takashi stood close to the awakening survivor, slumped in a chair toward the back of the runabout. Wade watched from a distance as Virgil tried to speak. "Virgil," he said hoarsely. He never liked being called Dr. Reed. It always made him feel older than his twenty-eight years.

Samara turned to Takashi. "Why don't you get Virgil a drink of water," she asked him. As Takashi dutifully scrambled to the front of the vehicle, Samara sat next to the man. "I know you're a little disoriented. So, before you talk, let me explain some things." Takashi returned with a whole bottle of water which she gingerly placed into the Doctor's hands. "Drink this." She helped to bring it to his lips. His throat was still dry, and he choked a bit as he greedily gulped it down.

"Thank you," he said.

"My name is Samara Lewynn," she started, then pointed to Takashi. "This is Takashi Tanimoto," then to Wade. "And he's Wade Fassell." We're from the NTSS Magellan, your supply ship.

Virgil nodded. He recognized the names, if not the faces, having never met any of these people in person.

"When we arrived today, there was no response from your

survey team," Samara continued. "We came to investigate and found you." She took a second to consider her next statement. "You were… attached to a creature…"

"A paraxion," Virgil informed them in a matter-of-fact tone.

"Which is a what, exactly?" asked Wade, moving closer to the group.

Virgil put down the empty bottle in his hands and rubbed his forehead. He suddenly appeared consumed with grief as his eyes reddened. This discussion was proving painful for him to continue.

"Tell us about them," Samara asked inquisitively.

Her manner appeared to be working. Virgil collected himself, exhaling loudly. "Well, there's not much to tell," he started, almost lost in his head. "Indigenous to this area, relatively docile organism… curious." He suddenly stopped and locked eyes with Samara. "You say I was harvested by it?" he asked almost casually.

"Ummm… yeah," Samara offered. "You were attached to it." It was the only way she could describe what she had seen.

"It figures," he said dejectedly. "You see…silly me. I thought I was back at Theta Colony Station putting together a rescue mission."

Takashi looked at Samara and shrugged. What the hell was this guy talking about? Theta Colony Station was in another galaxy and more than a week away, at minimum. That is, if you were lucky enough to be on a ship with sub-light drives.

"I'm sorry, Virgil. "We're a little confused," said Samara.

"Sure," came Virgil's reply. "The paraxions, well, they've got this special trick, you see. If they get a hold of you, they pump you full of venom, which places you in a coma." His breathing began to speed up as his anxiety again started to rise. His eyes darted around the small cabin as he continued his erratic explanation. "Fuckin' trippy. All types of hallucinations. The thing must have gotten me, and I never realized it. Eventually, it would have dropped me when it was moving on and left me there for it to wear off. Who knows how long it might have been, though."

He then focused his attention back on Samara. "I was getting help." Suddenly, something clicked in his head, and the venom-induced haze he had been in abruptly ended. The full extent of his situation smacked him in the face, and he bolted from his seat, once again awash with panic. "Oh, Shit. Nara. Oh, God. We've got to go back for her!" Wade instinctively reached for his gun in case this drug-addled lunatic crossed the line. "What day is it?" Virgil demanded. They all looked at him, speechless. Where was he going with this? Virgil suddenly grabbed Takashi by the shoulders. "What day is it?!" he repeated.

Takashi hesitated before answering. "Ahh... The eighth. It's the eighth."

Letting go of the young man, Virgil did the math in his head, and his eyes went wide. "That's two days!" he declared. "Fucking two days!"

"Get it together, Doc," Wade interjected. "You're not making any sense."

Virgil was in his own little mad world as a look of horror gripped him. "I left her over ten days ago." He turned to Samara for help that she had no way of giving. "Ten days. I promised her I'd bring help."

"Virgil. Listen to me," instructed Samara. "The base camp is gone. We've been there. There's nothing left."

"I hallucinated, in detail, an entire two weeks of my life. As if things had progressed from the point I was harvested. I can't even tell what's real anymore." Said Virgil. "Are you real? Is this all real? Maybe you're just what I imagined the Samara

Lewynn from the ship manifests would be like. The savior my subconscious knew I needed. I don't know."

Virgil shook his head as he slumped back into his chair. "No. I know where the base camp is. *That* part is real." he informed them. "And we're going to go find it and save my sister." Virgil's manner shifted from upset to cold determination as Samara looked to Wade, wondering just what the hell they were dealing with.

ΔΔΔ

Aden strolled the long corridor that ran the length of his ship, lost in thought. He felt terrible about how he handled the situation with Panya. Now, having all the information, her behavior, as odd as it was, made some modicum of sense. Still, there was no excuse or room for her deception, which would be dealt with as soon as they returned to Dock 85a. Aden dreaded the thought of having to find another Comms Officer. He was just getting comfortable with Panya and considered himself lucky to find someone as competent as she was — and she *was* qualified, if green. The pickings were slim these days, especially at Dock 85a, which was not exactly the hub for quality crew. It might be worth putting a crew posting on the UniWeb now to find a preliminary candidate before their return. It might also give the kind of candidate with a little more ambition time to travel to Dock 85 and meet them there on their arrival.

Unfortunately, he had this business to deal with now. What a pain. As he reached Panya's door, he paused, then knocked. The sound of rustling inside preceded the door opening.

Awakened from sleep, it took Panya a moment to focus her eyes on the captain. "Sir?"

"You got rid of it?" asked the captain.

Still groggy, it took her a minute to realize what he was referring to. Did he know that not only was she pregnant, but she was considering aborting her baby? Would Samara have betrayed her trust and told the captain about her personal business? As the haze of sleep dissipated, Panya suddenly zeroed in on what he was asking -- it was about the creature she had been told to take outside. She stumbled to answer. "Yeah."

Aden studied her curious behavior. Was she lying to him? No, she wouldn't be that stupid. He chalked it up to her pregnancy, remembering all the odd and forgetful behaviors his wife experienced when they had their first child. "Look, Panya," he started. "I know I was short with you, but you have got to understand that I have more than just you to worry about." He felt like he was playing the father figure again. Ironically, Panya would be roughly the age of his daughter Hera had she lived past her first birthday.

Panya's eyes dropped, unable to match his stare.

He looked past her into her tiny room and noticed a small med packet atop a shelf. Probably prenatal vitamins, he thought. He continued, "We don't do things here that could needlessly jeopardize the crew's lives. Understood?"

"I understand, sir."

"I certainly hope so," he replied. "Everything you do has consequences that affect you and the people around you."

She nodded. Aden *was* right, which made her feel worse for lying to him.

"That's all." Aden started to reach for her to give her a fatherly pat on the shoulder but restrained himself. This was not his daughter but an officer under his charge. Keep it all business. Otherwise, she'll never learn.

As he disappeared down the corridor, Panya backed into her room and slowly closed the door behind her. She then focused her attention on something struggling with a blanket on the floor. "Don't worry, you're safe here," she said lovingly to the tiny creature holding its tiny hands up to her.

ΔΔΔ

The door slid open as Aden entered his quarters. He looked at his watch and rubbed his eyes. It had already been a long day, and it wasn't over yet. Looking at the unmade bed, he paused. Lying on the far side of the sheets was a pile of crumpled clothes. Crossing to the bed, he sat down, letting his hand rifle through Samara's laundry. Finding her panties, he gently lifted them up in his hand. The fabric was silky to the touch, much like the feel of Samara's skin. He thought about how much he needed her in his life and how she kept him going, even when her love for him turned sour. He missed the days when things were simple, but those days were long gone.

The comm-link in his quarters crackled with static as Oliver's voice invaded his private moment. "Captain, we're receiving a transmission from the ground team."

Aden dropped the panties back in the pile. "Patch it through."

A moment later, the monitor on his wall blinked to life as Samara's sculpted young face peered back at him. She wore her protective mask of emotional indifference that he had grown to know so well and seen so often as the days trudged forward. "Captain," she began formally. "There have been some interesting developments. Dr. Reed will fill you in."

Before Aden could even react to the mention of the stranger, Samara shifted away from the lens on her end, and Virgil's face appeared on the screen. "Captain Harker, I'm Dr. Virgil Reed, survey team exobiologist. We have had a very unfortunate situation that has led to the destruction of our base camp and the death of most of our team."

"Go on," replied Aden.

"Unbeknown to us at the time, we had set up camp on the hind region of a nearly mature adult land strider." Aden knew little of the local wildlife, so he nodded, assuming the information he needed would be forthcoming. "Prior to full maturation, they hibernate for what we understand to be hundreds of years," continued Virgil. "About two weeks ago, ours awoke. According to our research, to complete its reproductive cycle, it must travel to and submerge itself in the Zumerian Sea to spawn. That's where it's headed. Time is of utmost importance."

"Time for what?" asked the captain.

"There are members of the ground team still trapped on the land strider."

Aden stood up and paced before the monitor. "But you said it's been about two weeks—"

"I know these creatures, this planet," insisted Virgil. "There's still a solid chance."

"Aren't these the things that are supposed to be the size of a mountain?" inquired Aden. "What do you expect to happen when you do find it?"

Virgil was not expecting this kind of resistance, which ruffled his composure. He led his small group of bio-scientists as part of the more extensive Vega Prime Survey Team and was not used to being questioned. "You're just going to have to trust me." He said.

"I'm not questioning your expertise," informed the captain. "But I think you should return to the Magellan and brief the crew first."

"But—"

Samara grabbed the vidcom from her end and swung it, so it faced her. "You can't just give up on these people," she said with a hint of irritation.

"I'm not giving up on them. We just need time to map out a plan." Said, Aden.

"We don't have time," Samara barked back. "It could be at the sea already, and the sun is going down."

Samara knew how to annoy him, and Aden was becoming increasingly frustrated by her clear inability to take a step back and look at things rationally. "That's my point. So why don't you get back here, and then we can do a fly-by?"

"And what if it's in a no-fly zone, or a distortion pocket moves into the area, and we have to wait? Then what?" asked Samara combatively. "It's four hours back to the Magellan as it is. If we can at least lock in on its coordinates, we can have Mech map out a potential flight route. The Sea's got plenty of flyable zones, especially in the west.

"Dammit, Samara, stop being so goddamn stubborn!"

The gloves were off. "Fuck you, Aden! Why don't you stop acting like a tired old man?" Samara clicked off the comm and stormed out of the runabout. Aden shook his head and pondered his next move as the screen on the wall went black.

∆∆∆

Standing near the rim of the enormous pit, Samara's eyes focused on the far edge where it broke through the forest and left an enormously wide opening in the vegetation line. She took in the scale of what must have been the creature's burrow. As Virgil had described, she imagined something so massive that life teemed on its very back — plants, trees, wildlife — all of it.

She knew snapping at Aden was counterproductive, but she just couldn't control her temper right now. She felt squeezed between Wade and their new acquaintance Virgil as they bickered like little boys, posturing for dominance. Staring into the depths of the chasm below, it was easy to take a step back and realize that she had been making things worse, but in the heat of the moment, she just couldn't see it as clearly as she did now. She added this latest incident to her mental list of regrets and started to think again about the land strider.

The sound of approaching footsteps snapped her out of her thoughts. It was probably Wade coming to lecture her about the chain of command for the umpteenth time. She was surprised not only by the message but by the messenger as well. "We've got the go-ahead," said Virgil. "Tomorrow, first light."

"How did you convince him?" she asked, slightly suspicious and wanting to know more.

"It was Wade," he answered. "He agreed with you."

"That's a first," she responded sarcastically. It might as well have been true. Wade never took her side, even if he agreed with her. It was something he took devilish pride in. How could they remain in competition for Aden's right hand if they suddenly started agreeing with each other?

Samara looked up at the twilight sky. Virgil moved closer to her and joined in on the stargazing. "I've been studying this planet so long that I sometimes forget to look up at the stars and appreciate the view."

Deep down, he wondered if his tunnel vision, his *obsession* with studying Vega Prime superseded what was truly important in life. This day was a slap in the face that he needed. A test. A reminder that things can change at a moment's notice and that if you don't appreciate the now, you are doomed to a long life of regret and despair.

Why did he stop looking up at the stars? As a young boy on Earth, that's all he did. That's all he wanted. To journey to the stars and explore, but now that he had his wish, he truly wanted Nara and to be back at home on Earth where everything was safe and made sense.

"When Nara and I first got here, we would make up our own constellations," he said, pointing to the heavens. "That bright one there, next to the cluster of three stars. I call that *Asteria*," he said with a smirk. "It's Latin for *star*." He looked to Samara for some reaction, but she didn't get it. "It's sort of a joke."

Samara turned to him, her face void of emotion. "Can I ask you something?" She had something far more important on her mind than the categorization of constellations in the Vega System.

"Sure," Virgil answered.

"Why in God's name would you waste your time in a place like this?" said Samara bitingly.

Virgil tried not to take the attack personally. "I don't consider this a waste of my time," he explained calmly. "What we're doing here is important."

Samara needed to vent, and Virgil was easy pickings. "In six years, you haven't figured out anything. It seems to me you've just collected a lot of assumptions and conjecture."

"You've got to start somewhere," said Virgil, forcing a smile. "That's the beginnings of the scientific method."

"But what are you trying to accomplish besides getting yourselves all killed?"

"Samara, this is what humanity is all about, the search for knowledge… for universal truth. Sometimes knowledge for its own sake or the sake of the simple but profound evolution of the collective understanding of our species is the goal." He was amazed that he had to explain this to her. "Communication with another species. We're trying to unlock the mysteries of the universe." His blood was pumping again as his own words reminded him exactly why he was on Vega Prime and not cowering back on Earth. No one expanded their mind by playing it safe. No one ever did anything worthwhile by sitting at home, afraid to explore the world around them. He realized at that moment that he, Dr. Virgil Reed, had looked up to the stars for adventure and not only found it but embraced it with all his heart and soul. It was here on Vega Prime that he built his new home, and even better, his beloved sister Nara was right by his side.

"But as far as you know, these are just... animals," she insisted. "You might as well ask your dog if he knows the meaning of life."

Virgil studied her momentarily. How naive was this woman? He almost felt sorry for her. But he would be the bigger man and would enlighten her. Make her understand how mistaken she was. "Let me show you something that might change your mind."

CHAPTER EIGHT

Aden sat on the edge of his bunk contemplating the events of the day. His hand went to his temples and massaged the tension building behind them. As he dropped them back onto his lap, he flexed them and then tightened them into fists. These once strong hands were weakening as he got older, much like his resolve. He could feel one in the slight hints of joint pain and the other fraying at the edge of his being. Pulling back the sheets, he slid under the covers and hit the lights, leaving himself alone in the darkness.

△△△

In the alien forest, two small lights penetrated the blackness. They belonged to Mech, who illuminated a path through the woods wide enough for Virgil and Samara to walk at a reasonable pace. Virgil had transformed yet again — now fleet of mind and of foot, he had to fight the urge to run ahead of Samara.

"We found the object while searching for McMasters," informed Virgil.

Samara responded impatiently, "Is it much farther?"

"Just up ahead," he reassured. He knew that where they were going was well worth the trudge. He couldn't wait to see the look on her smug face when she saw it. He wanted to savor the moments she stood there in slack-jawed awe. The thought of it invigorated him as they pushed further into the night.

"Christ. Aden would laugh if he knew what we were doing right now." Samara chuckled.

"Why's that?"

"He used to drag me out hiking all the time. I hated it," she said. "I'm more of a homebody." She almost had to convince herself of this last part. Why else would she have spent a good part of her life holed up in the space freighter that was her home if she wasn't?

"That's a shame," responded Virgil. He loved the outdoors and couldn't understand why most people insisted on staying indoors when there was so much to discover on the worlds they lived on. "It's good to commune with nature."

"That wasn't his reason."

"Then what was?" he asked.

"He said it reminded him of the old days," she answered ironically.

"Well, that's good."

"Not if you knew what he did back then." Samara didn't bother to expound on her answer, and Virgil decided not to press her. He would get to know this captain on his own terms. They continued in silence. Virgil thought about the pleasures he had experienced in the numerous landscapes that he had explored during his lifetime, while Samara considered the troubled past that still haunted the man she most desperately loved.

△△△

Aden lay in the dark cabin, eyes straining to stay open as he drifted off. A single word on his lips breathlessly escaped as he surrendered to his exhaustion.

Samara.

Enemy fire exploded all around Aden. Decked out in full combat gear, there was a look of panic in his eye as the world erupted in flames around him. He had to find safety. He had to find a place where they wouldn't find him. Even the blackness of night wasn't enough to shroud him.

The Mallix Conflict had gotten out of control. What was left of his Troop Commander was strewn about a nearby ditch along with most of what was his squad. A rogue Golodoth infantry unit had taken them by complete surprise, and it was a massacre. Aden just barely escaped the carnage with the enemy squad hot on his heels, blanketing the area with shrapnel bombs and thermal grenades. If there was one thing the Golodoths loved, it was their antipersonnel weapons. It was only a matter of time before they found him. Unlike the others, he would probably be taken prisoner. Tortured. Examined. He had heard the stories -- the Golodoths knew nothing of human anatomy or endurance, and they didn't care. They would extract information in any way necessary, no matter how many limbs were crushed or vital organs seared along the way.

As another blast lit up the immediate area Aden saw the devastated husk of a building in the distance. There was sanctuary if he could just make it. His thought was interrupted by the familiar howl of the Golodoth troopers closing the distance behind him. These bulky bipedal humanoid creatures looked like they had stepped out of a nightmare. Every bit of them was covered in armor fashioned for extreme warfare. Their helmets offered only a glimpse of their disturbingly grotesque heads and faces. White leathery skin mottled with veins stretched tightly over bony features. Rows of sharp teeth lined their gaping mouths, and two cloudy dead eyes gave no sign of what the creatures were thinking. They had no pity. Probably didn't even understand the concept.

Fortunately for Aden, they hadn't seen him, and though they continued toward his general direction, they seemed slow-moving and more random than meticulous. He threw himself into the blown-out building and took refuge in the piles of debris that filled the interior. Fatigued, he slumped against a wall, his back now covered and the rest of him obscured by piles of trash and rubble. He was scared. Completely lost. Hopeless. With no way of communicating with the base, he was on his own. It was only a matter of time before they found him. Is this how his family, his beloved wife and child had suffered when the Golodoths came for them? Were they strong in the face of terror? Were they stronger than him?

He slowly raised the barrel of his field pistol to his temple. Maybe they'd understand when he saw them on the other side. Maybe they'd just be so happy to see him and would forgive his cowardice. Maybe he wouldn't be frightened anymore.

His finger tightened on the trigger as the world went silent.

There was the sound of shifting metal. Had they found him so soon?

He heard a whimper. Not a howl like the maniacal Golodoths, but a pained cry. The painful cry of a young girl.

"Please... Help me." It sounded muffled. Entombed. "Help me," came the disembodied voice again.

"Hello?" Said Aden tentatively, still poised to end it all. "Is somebody there?" He thought he might be crazy, hallucinating from the fear.

"Please... Help..."

He shook his head as he dropped his arm, then holstering his pistol, he got up and moved toward the origin of the sound. "I'm here," he called out. "Keep talking so I can find you."

"I'm trapped. I can't move." came the panicked reply. "You have to help me."

"Stay calm. I'm going to help you," he reassured her. Something caught his eye in the rubble. Trapped underneath a fallen piece of furniture was a frightened young girl. She must have been in her teens. Her skin was chocolate brown. Her face was angelic. "What's your name?" he said to her as he positioned himself by the heavy wall unit pinning her to the ground.

"Samara," she said.

"Samara. I'm Corporal Aden Harker," he said. "I'm gonna help you." Using what was left of his strength, Aden heaved the unit upwards. She yelped as the metal pinched into her legs, but a moment later she was free. Shoving the unit aside, Aden faced Samara, who immediately threw herself into his arms. It had been so long since he had been hugged like this, and it gave him the strength that he believed he no longer had. His family would have to wait for him another day.

"Let's get out of here," he said to her. As he stood up, an explosion erupted behind him, hurling him and Samara like rag dolls across the room. Once again, the world turned black.

ΔΔΔ

Aden woke up a week later to find himself at a field hospital with his wounds now cleaned and dressed and well on his way to a full recovery. Still hazy, it took his mind a few moments to process. He was alive. But what about the girl? What was her name? Samara. Yes, it was Samara. Had she perished in the explosion? His answer came quickly. As he turned to his left, he noticed someone curled up, gently sleeping in a nearby chair. It was her. "Samara," he attempted, but his voice was dry and scratchy. The word was barely audible.

Somehow, she heard. Her head slowly lifted from the chair, and she stared at him and smiled. "Welcome back, corporal," she said as tears welled up in her eyes. She crossed to the bed to be closer to him.

"We're alive," he said with difficulty.

"You saved us," she replied. She poured some water from a small dispenser in the wall, then brought it to him. He was shaky, still disoriented. She helped him drink the cool liquid and watched as the lights started to come on behind his eyes.

As his head cleared, Aden looked around the small hospital room. There were other wounded soldiers. Most worse off than he was. He turned back to Samara. "I want to go home."

"Me too," she said and laid her head on his chest.

ΔΔΔ

They kept Aden in the hospital for a few more days before they were satisfied with his condition. On the day of his discharge, Commander Hollister stopped by and awarded him a valor commendation and thanked him for his bravery. Aden played the dutiful soldier and accepted it without incident, but inside he felt that it was unearned, and it shamed him to be distinguished like that. He alone knew what had happened in the moments before he had "earned" it. Later he gave it to Samara. She was far more deserving to his mind, having survived in a war zone without the benefit of the years of training and top-of-the-line tactical gear he had. She impressed him in a way that only survivors who have recognized each other as such can. That and their shared experience connected them even more deeply than many of his so-called "brothers-in-arms." With no family left, she had wound up at Aden's side. With none of his own left, he was glad to have her there.

Upon leaving the hospital, they journeyed to a nearby holo-cemetery where Samara said farewell to her parents, who had died a week before Aden discovered her in the wreckage that day. The two of them were now beholden to each other, both orphans in a way. They would make their new home together far away from planet Nebali and the waning days of the conflict.

Aden made Samara a promise that day that he would take care of her. Protect her and, most importantly, never leave her. She made him that promise too. Neither of them thought about the dark places that promise might one day lead to.

They returned to Earth for a while and moved into Aden's condo. She found odd jobs to help pay the bills while Aden convalesced over the next year or so. Samara was now almost eighteen and had never really seen the universe. She was also beginning to show signs of restlessness. With the Mallix Conflict resolved, interstellar travel was once again picking up, and the deals were too good to pass up. As soon as he was fully healed, Aden sold off the condo as well as most of his worldly possessions and the two of them left Earth for the last time.

After a year of travel, money was beginning to run thin, and it became clear that they *both* needed to find work. Because many starships were still being retrofitted for post-war use, there was an abundance of work in maintenance and repair. Aden took a position as a grease monkey in the Berillion shipyards and was able to swing Samara a job as his trainee and assistant.

Samara was always a bit of a tomboy, even before she met Aden, and she enjoyed the work. By that time, even dressed down and covered in oil, she looked ravishing. It didn't go unnoticed by Aden how the other dock workers gazed at her or tried to make passes at her as she grew into herself.

Samara seemed okay with it, almost like she enjoyed some of it. Her cavalier attitude about flirting did eventually wear Aden down. He had become increasingly protective of her over their time together, and unbeknown to her, he had a "friendly chat" with some of the fellows after one of the shifts he worked solo. A couple of broken bones and some missing teeth later, most of them got the message: Look, but don't touch.

Neither of them was happy to stay in one place too long. Aden and Samara eventually moved on, working at various docks across the Traxon Quadrant. Aden moved up in the ranks to chief engineer, and Samara displayed her growing abilities in the sciences along the way. Soon she grew tired of always being covered in filth and muck, and when a premed nurse training position opened up at the dock medical unit, she took it. Aden was pleased by the decision. He figured between the two of them, they could fix just about anything, whether it be mechanical or flesh and blood.

Time went by, Aden moved further up the ranks, and Samara moved from trainee to school and doing exceptionally well to boot. Things were good.

∆∆∆

Samara's twenty-first birthday was upon them, and Aden wanted to do something special. He had tracked down a recipe for Samara's favorite dish, Tidellax Monk Rube, and did his best to recreate it at home. Unfortunately, his knife skills were a tad rusty, and he managed to slice his finger in ways that Samara hadn't witnessed before. She chided him for his carelessness as the crimson flowed freely, then Samara's nursing skills kicked into gear, and she was on him with her med kit in seconds.

Aden compressed a kitchen rag tightly around the wounded index finger. "I think it's pretty bad." He looked like a little boy as he held it out to her.

"Let me take a better look," she said gently. "They always look worse than they are." Like the professional she had become, she evaluated the injury and dressed the wound. Three adhesive stitches and some dermal glue held it closed. Still holding onto his hand, she finished wrapping the site of the wound up. "See.

Mommy made it all better." Playfully, she kissed the bandage. Aden tried a smile but was growing a tad concerned when she lingered a little long with the kiss. He retracted his hand and then tried to cover for the awkwardness. "Thank you," he stumbled. "It feels better already." She could see from his cheeks she had him. He could see in her eyes he was caught.

She smiled coyly. "Why are you acting so funny?"

"No reason," he replied unconvincingly with that same little boy look.

"I can tell when you're lying," she said playfully as she moved in closer. "What is it you're not telling me?" She looked him square in the eyes, searching.

He looked deeply conflicted. This was a new one for Samara. In all the time she knew Aden, he was extremely decisive. When he made up his mind, he did it. Hell, he was almost as stubborn as she was. This was not like him at all. Was he afraid of her, of her being this close to him? The moment excited her, and she wanted to see how far she could push it. "Is it a secret?" she said seductively.

Aden felt the edge of the counter press against his lower spine. He was out of room to wiggle away. Trapped. She pressed her mouth close to his ear. "I thought we had no secrets," she whispered lovingly.

As her lips gently kissed his neck, he could only say one word.

Samara

CHAPTER NINE

Arms crossed, Samara stood next to Mech in a small clearing as Virgil trotted over to her. He smiled mischievously. "Prepare to be amazed." Turning, he excitedly rushed beyond a patch of tentacle-like vegetation, like a stage act disappearing behind the curtain. Thousands of strands hung from what looked like the branches of what Samara thought of as trees. They swayed and moved — not from the motion of the air but to some internal rhythm. Occasionally, one would light up, its chemical luminescence in stark white contrast to the deep blue of the other tendrils.

He certainly was putting on a show for her -- and she was beginning to tire of it -- but she had come this far. A few more minutes could be endured to get it over with. The whole affair seemed important to Virgil, so she was willing to attempt to understand it, even if it was to better understand him in her capacity as the ship's medic.

"Mech, lead the way to Dr. Reed," she instructed the robot. Mech dutifully obeyed, clearing a path ahead of her while simultaneously keeping a steady beam of light before them and on the ground. The last thing she wanted to do was trip on the uneven alien soil or get tangled in those weird tendrils. Falling flat on her face would certainly mar her condescending look of indignation when she finally saw the blasted thing that Virgil was so hot and heavy for.

As Mech broke through the last foliage, they were suddenly engulfed in a blanket of light. She shielded her eyes to block the rays that bounced and refracted, creating a cascade of white shards dancing on her. It was an amplified reflection of Mech's lights. "Mech, turn down the lights," she commanded. As their intensity waned, so did the glow causing her to squint. Blinking fast, she finally adjusted her sight to the spectacle before her.

A massive sculpture of crystal-clear resin stretched across a clear area of the forest. Running at least a couple of hundred feet long, its glassy spires reached up to the heavens over thirty feet high. Its scope and beauty were, to Virgil, an overwhelming vision of wonder and glory.

At first glance, the sculpture appeared to have no definite design scheme, just a conglomeration of shapes huddled together here and spread out over there. Upon further inspection, definite forms disclosed themselves both without and within the object. Those forms used the shape and structure of the object and what appeared to be finely detailed bubbles and colored resins trapped inside to reveal their tableau.

With a furrowed brow, Samara approached the structure. Her hand came to rest on a human-like shape amidst the typhoon of bizarre objects within. "This… this is a *person*," she spoke, barely able to get the words out.

"Yeah," Virgil confirmed gleefully. "*Isn't it incredible?*" This was precisely the reaction he was hoping for. As far as he was concerned, this was a significant victory against the cynics of the universe. He pointed to another area of the vast object. He had her in the palm of his hands, and he might as well maximize the moment. "Now look at this," he instructed.

Before him was a representation of a solar system, colored globes were suspended in place inside the resin. Circular lines intersected each sphere and suggested their orbit around the star at its center, which had tendrils that jutted out from its surface. The whole image hung in space.

Samara noticed that the third planet from the sun was

different from the rest. It had details that the others lacked: Continents. Islands. Oceans. "Is that the Earth?"

"Yes," said Virgil. This reminded Virgil of when he briefly taught at Forma-U. She had that same wide-eyed look that his young students had as he showed them the secret wonders of the universe. It gave him a rush. So many of his studies and discoveries over the years were never appreciated or downplayed by his uptight colleagues, who were too egomaniacal to share the spotlight. Today he had a rapt audience (albeit of only one) who could truly appreciate his life's work. He watched her with keen interest as she studied the find of the century, amused by her inability to process this new information fully.

"Did you build this?" she asked.

Virgil was almost too incredulous to respond. "No," he stammered, "I told you, *we found it.*"

"But..."

He stopped her before she could continue. "Something *here*, something *on this planet,* made this and left it for us to find," he explained. "*It wants to communicate with us.*"

Samara took another long look at the crystalline sculpture peppered with many things intrinsic only to Earth. "But how does it know all of this?" she asked, starting to sound generally concerned. She moved to another part of the sculpture and pointed it out to him. The translucent shape vaguely resembled a primate perched on a tree. "This is a gorilla," she said adamantly. "There aren't gorillas here." Her tone was laced with hostility as she pointed to the resin tree. "And the tree...that's an Earth tree." She then turned to him. The look in her eyes was no longer awe and amazement but something altogether different: fear and mistrust. "I'm right about this, aren't I?"

Virgil didn't like this at all. His star pupil had abruptly turned on him, and it was going downhill fast. Now it was his turn for confusion. He didn't understand why she was acting so alarmed.

"About what?"

"This isn't incredible, Virgil. It's terrifying."

"You're overreacting," he said with a forced smile while trying to diffuse her misplaced anger. "Think about the majesty and simplicity of this message. Whoever it was is showing us things that we know and can relate to. It wants us to know that it understands us."

"But you understand nothing," she quickly retorted.

Virgil was genuinely stunned at her about-face. This was the reaction that he had least expected. In the little time Virgil had been around her, he thought he had Samara figured out. He had prepared himself for indifference and a lack of understanding, but this was just plain paranoia and lunacy as far as he was concerned. "How can you read danger from something so benign? So beautiful?"

"To assume that this is benevolent is *ludicrous,* doctor." Samara was losing her patience with Virgil, and she could feel one of her "moments" bubbling to the surface. She quickly reminded herself that she barely knew him and held back on the urge to explain it like he was a child. Samara told herself to be in the moment and not judge. She bit her lip hard and tasted the salty blood in her mouth as Virgil continued.

"You're missing the bigger picture," he informed her. "Whatever this is, it's a sign of cognitive intelligence. This proves that we *can* and *will* communicate with what's here." His heart was racing. He didn't like having his theories questioned. He had had enough of that in the past and had made a concerted effort not to let anyone belittle him or his ideas again. He took a deep breath. "You wanted to know why I would waste my time on this planet. *You're looking at it.*" He thrust a finger at the sculpture. "If it weren't for *this*, I would have given up years ago."

Samara shook her head. "Well, I hope when you find your answer, it's worth it." She turned around and headed back toward the runabout, with Mech catching up to lead the way. They didn't bother waiting for Virgil.

△△△

The sun beat down on the runabout as it followed the large trench at the far side of the crater. Stretching toward the horizon, the valley seemed to go on forever. At the wheel, Wade kept the truck on course. Next to him sat Virgil, anxiety on his face. The others were in the back running routine diagnostic checks. Takashi poked his head into the cockpit. "Meg has a lock on something ahead," he informed them. "It's big."

In the distance, a mammoth land strider headed toward the Zumerian Sea, its gigantic tail burrowing a trench into the beach. The monster had an enormous back that spanned literal miles. Four legs supported the structure, bending at odd angles. Accenting the legs were oversized feet that crushed the ground beneath them as it lumbered across the planet's surface. The creature's head, a sightless mass of tough flesh with a wide gaping mouth, rocked back and forth as it moved. The bellow emitted from its mouth caused the ground to vibrate. Even the teal-colored gelatinous sea trembled from the sound and retracted its shoreline.

△△△

Aden, Oliver, and Panya stared, fixated on the large display at the front of the cockpit, which showed a live feed of the land strider closing in on the Sea. Takashi appeared in an inset window at the top right corner. "Are you getting this, sir?" he inquired.

"Yeah. We see it," responded the captain. The creature was bigger than he imagined. It was like watching an entire city slowly moving across the landscape.

"So far, it looks like a clear flight zone above -- for the moment," continued Takashi. "Meg's mapping out a list of potential flight plans, but we may have to re-approach Prime from space to get to them."

"What about survivors?" asked Aden. He was hoping this wasn't a fool's errand.

Wade appeared next. "Nothing yet," said the XO. "We're going to maneuver closer--" The screen suddenly flickered as static erupted. The images and sound reappeared a moment later as they caught the end of Wade's sentence. "--if we do."

"Wade, come again," said Aden. "We just had a transmission glitch. Come again, Wade."

Oliver and Panya headed to their workstations to try to assess what had just happened.

Wade repeated his prior statement. "I said that we're going to—" There was another burst of static, and then the Magellan suddenly lurched. Aden gripped his chair and held on as a sound like trees snapping filled the bridge. As the noise approached, the din in the cabin became unbearable. Panya covered her ears to muffle the sound.

Wade finally appeared on the monitor again. "Sir, you're breaking up."

Aden was forced to yell over the noise to be heard. "Stand by Wade. Something's going on." The screen went to static as something substantial smashed into the hull, pitching the crew against the inside walls. Aden turned to his chief engineer. "Outside monitor!" The static-filled screen dissolved, revealing the exterior of Vega Prime. For a moment, they saw only trees, then a massive shape filled their view and pressed against the

Magellan, causing the ship to rock violently on its landing gear. "Hang on!" yelled Aden to his crew.

ΔΔΔ

Inside the runabout, the ground team searched each other's faces for answers. Wade looked at Takashi, who instinctively turned to the Mech.

"Meg. Please scan the Zumerian Sea and our immediate surroundings for electromagnetic or other anomalous interference," Takashi instructed.

The robot took a moment, then replied, "Negative."

Samara didn't know what to say. "Do you think they're in trouble?"

Nobody answered. They were as baffled as she was. As Wade steered the runabout closer to the land strider, they waited patiently for more information from their mother ship. None was forthcoming.

"It's probably nothing," Virgil offered unconvincingly.

Wade needed facts, not conjecture. "Could something attack the Magellan?" he asked Virgil, the resident expert on all things Vega Prime.

Virgil responded nervously, "Why would anything do that?"

"I don't know," responded Wade. "That's why I'm asking *you*. Didn't some of these creatures attack your camp?"

"That was different," said Virgil. "They panicked when the strider began moving," he then mistakenly added. "You wouldn't understand."

Wade slammed on the breaks, pitching everyone forward. That was the final straw.

"Why are you stopping?" demanded Virgil.

Turning to the young scientist, Wade got in his face and gave him a piece of his mind. "I could give a shit about what you think I can understand. Our ship might be in danger, and you're the only one who knows about this place." He paused for emphasis. "So, when I ask your opinion, I want a straight answer. *Is there anything here capable of attacking the Magellan?*"

Virgil looked around the cabin uncomfortably. All eyes were on him. He was holding back valuable information, and they all knew it. It was probably best if he came clean. "Yes," he answered reluctantly.

"Thank you," replied Wade as he revved up the truck's engines and cut the wheel to the left. Virgil panicked as the runabout took an abrupt U-turn away from the land strider. "What are you *doing*?! We're not done yet!" They were there to save his sister and the rest of the team. What was the point of turning back now? If the Magellan was in danger, they could do nothing anyway. "Go back," he pleaded.

"I don't want to hear from you until I ask you a question. Understood?" The vein in Wade's forehead was throbbing. Samara thought she was the only one capable of making the XO that angry.

Virgil grit his teeth. He turned to see the land strider speedily disappearing behind them. It was so close to the Sea. There was not much time left. His sister Nara needed him. He promised her that he'd come back and save her. Virgil suddenly lunged for the side door and flung it open. A second later, he hurled himself from the speeding vehicle and tumbled onto the ground below, rolling away to disperse the impact of the leap.

"Wade!" Samara called Wade's attention to the escape. Through the open door, they watched Virgil as he got up and raced back toward the giant creature looming in the distance. "We gotta stop him!" yelled Samara as she leaped from the vehicle and chased after him.

Wade was not expecting her to act so quickly or decisively. "Samara! Get back in here!" he called out, slamming on the brakes again. Before he could yell out to her again, a garbled message erupted through the comm-link static. It was Aden. "Mayday! Mayday! This is the NTSS Magellan. We are under attack!"

△△△

Outside, a monstrous slug-like creature about a third of the size of the ship had pounded the Magellan broadside. When it reared up, it showed a distended midsection with transparent gooey sacs embedded all over its underbelly. About a third of the way back from its head, two long tentacle-like appendages that ended in small openings searched the ship's surface for a grip. Its head was nearly round, surrounded by evil-looking mouths in a ring around its circumference. The top was boney, shell-like, and hard. Like a wrecking ball, the slug bashed its head repeatedly against the ship's hull and gave it one hell of a beating.

Aden slammed against his captain's chair. Sliding in, he buckled himself in place and turned to the others. "Get yourselves strapped in. We gotta get the hell out of here."

Panya adjusted her seat restraints. "But what about the ground team?"

There was another blow to the ship, and Aden turned to the engineer. No words needed to be exchanged. Oliver opened a cover and flipped some switches, which started up the engines. "Initiating automatic emergency take-off," informed Oliver.

The Magellan's engines hummed with life as an impossibly hot fire brewed in their cores. As the sound produced by their powering up escalated, the creature became more aggressive. Without warning, it whipped its rear section at the ship's middle. A tail-like structure extended and stretched out far beyond the ability of any known animal's skin. Still growing in length, the elastic tail wrapped around the stern of the Magellan like a lasso. Tensing up, the wormlike creature drew the ship toward its body.

The Magellan began to buckle as the flight stick in Oliver's hand wrenched itself away. He turned to Aden, panic in his eyes. Nothing he was doing seemed to be working. "I think this fucking thing's got us."

"Fire the boosters," ordered the captain as a last-ditch effort. Not the wisest choice, but the only one left given their situation.

The booster engines exploded with white-hot ferocity, propelling the ship upwards, but the slug continued to hold fast, struggling against the force of the engines. A tug-of-war ensued, and it only took a few seconds for the creature to drag the ship back toward the surface of the landing pad.

"It's pulling us down..." yelled Oliver.

Still trapped in the beast's grip, the ship's engines sputtered as it smacked down hard on its landing gear and bucked. The weight was too much for the shock absorbers, blowing out most of the gear and causing them to collapse. Metal screeched against metal as the ship rocked once and then settled down, crushing what was left of the landing gear. The engines cut out automatically.

The bridge was a mess of blown-out circuitry. Wires hung from the ceiling, and small fires burned throughout the interior. All three crew members lay unconscious at their stations as the comm in the corner of the main screen crackled with static, and a fuzzy image of Wade appeared. "Come in, Magellan. Come in."

ΔΔΔ

Back on the runabout, Wade peered into the monitor on the dashboard, searching for any sign of life. "Aden?" He tried again. "Do you hear me?" Frustrated, he slammed his hand down hard on the console. "Dammit!"

Takashi looked out the open door, spying Samara and Virgil far in the distance. "This is crazy, Wade," said the young Tech Officer.

"I want you to take Mech and follow them."

"But…"

"Just do it, Takashi." Wade was in no mood to get into an argument right now. Things had gotten way out of his control, and he was past the breaking point. "Take the weapons, some food, and the long-range comms," instructed the XO in what was, for him, an abnormally calm tone.

Takashi was worried. He could handle the out-of-control, temper flying Wade, but this calm, almost creepy version frightened him. He tried to read the man's eyes, but they gave him nothing. What exactly was Wade planning to do? "You're going to come back for us, right?"

Wade turned back around in his seat and placed his hands on the steering controls. "You better get going," he said, unable to look the young man in the eyes.

Warily, Takashi paused before collecting the gear. A moment later, he found himself standing once again on the alien landscape as he watched his only way back to the Magellan drive off into the dense jungle.

CHAPTER TEN

Virgil sprinted toward the lumbering strider that towered before him. He was going to save his sister with their help or not. Samara was closing the distance behind him, desperate to stop him. Sweat poured down her face as she exerted herself near the limit of her physical abilities. Pushing herself even harder, she caught up and pounced. They tumbled forward, wrapped into each other, and bounced on the ground before coming to a stop. Powdery sand flew everywhere and stuck to their skin. They both lay panting on the ground, exhausted and gasping for air.

"I'm not going back without her," said Virgil, between gulps of air.

The loud roar of engines in the distance caught Samara's attention. She turned to see the runabout taking off into the forest. Silhouetted by the sun, two lone figures made their way toward them -- it was Takashi and the Mech. "I don't think that's a problem anymore," she replied. What the hell was going on? Where did Wade think he was going? She got up off the ground and dusted herself off. Reaching out her hand, she helped Virgil to his feet.

Virgil was satisfied that he had turned the tide of this little adventure in his favor. "We'll use the robot to get on the strider," he said with an air of authority.

Samara immediately got right in Virgil's face. "So, you're giving the orders now?"

"It makes the most sense," he said. "I know this place."

"You know shit," she barked at him. "That was stupid what you just did." She could not believe the impudence of this guy. He might just have signed all their death warrants, and he was acting like it was all in a day's work. In her mind, it was one thing to be myopic but entirely another to act like a complete ass. She appreciated his need to save his sister, but was Nara's life worth more than the others? Than hers? "I'll make the decisions." She said. "Understood?"

He nodded.

"Good. Now go give Takashi a hand," she ordered. As he rushed off to the approaching Tech Officer, she turned to the creature, which, with every passing minute, got closer to the Zumerian Sea.

△△△

The fires had died, and the command center was deathly quiet. Aden stirred in his seat. Groaning, he reached for the side of his head and winced when he touched a fresh wound. Wiping the blood on his shirt, Aden got up and crossed directly to Panya. Pulling her off the console, he patted her face to wake her. "Panya... Panya wake up," he said to her, increasing his volume until he got the desired result.

Begrudgingly, she eventually opened her eyes. "What..."

A clamor to their right signaled Oliver's return to consciousness. "I guess we're still alive," he said warily.

Aden assessed the damage to the bridge. "Barely."

Suddenly, Panya panicked. She bolted up and pushed past Aden.

"Hey?!" yelled the captain.

Racing through the door, she ran out of the bridge and

into the central corridor sprinting all the way back to her quarters. She waved her hand at the biometric door lock and slipped in through the sliding door before it was even fully open. Her room was in shambles; clothes were strewn everywhere, drawers hung open, and toiletries lay on the ground. She stood at the door, searching through the chaos. Movement in a pile of displaced garments suddenly caught her eye. Removing the shroud of clothes, she revealed the tiny altricion beneath. It snuggled between a sock and a sweatshirt sleeve. It appeared to be unharmed as it reached up to her. Gently picking it up, she held it close. "It's okay, baby," she reassured the creature.

A shape appeared behind her at the door. "Get back to the bridge," Aden ordered. "That thing's still outside."

Taken by surprise, she whipped around without thinking. Aden's eyes fell on the creature cradled in her arms. His reaction was immediate. "I told you to get that off my ship!" he yelled.

Panya shook her head. "No. It's not safe outside."

Aden desperately tried to control himself and not explode with rage. "When we get back to the colony, I want you gone," he said evenly. "I think it was a big mistake for you to take this assignment." He could feel the anger building up inside, but he managed to keep himself in check. "Especially given your situation."

"Don't you have *any* compassion?" said Panya.

"Yes, I do. That's why I think you should resign from your post before I fire you." The captain was through with this discussion. "Now, get to the bridge." He took a deep breath and let the tension flow from his body. "And keep that thing out of my sight."

Panya wisely didn't protest and slipped past the captain.

Dropping his head, Aden caught a reflection of himself in Panya's broken mirror lying on the floor. The shards of his face that stared back were worn out and tired.

Oliver watched as Panya entered the bridge fixated on the tiny organism in her arms. Didn't Panya get rid of that thing hours ago? A moment later, Aden entered behind her, looking like a man of pure business. It didn't take a mind reader to realize that something bad just went down.

"It's still out there, captain, and it's got a good grip on us, too," he informed Aden as the captain took his seat. "From what I can tell, the ship's still in fair working condition, give or take a few minor repairs. Engines check out — though I haven't test-fired them. Comms and scanners seem to be back up. The problems are all in power distribution. If we put a strain on the ship now, she'll just shift into emergency low-power mode, and we'll be stuck until we get the juice flowing again anyway."

"How much time?" asked Aden.

Oliver scratched his head as he thought out loud. "Well, if I had Mech...."

Aden uncharacteristically snapped at him. "You don't. So, how much time?"

"Three hours minimum," he replied quickly, eager to diffuse any displaced anger aimed at him.

"Well, get to it." came the order.

As Oliver headed back to the engineering console, Aden studied the slug on the screen. Knowing nothing of this bizarre creature, he was at a complete loss. "What's that thing doing out there?" he pondered rhetorically.

"As far as I know... nothing," responded Oliver assuming that his opinion was required.

"What?" asked Aden, having not expected the reply.

"It's doing nothing."

△△△

Having exited the trench, the runabout now passed familiar ground. Maneuvering toward the trail they'd cut on their way to the crater, Wade headed back in the direction of the Magellan. This was the right decision; he was sure of it.

Panya's voice came through the comm. "Ground team, this is the Magellan. Come in."

"Go for the ground team," responded Wade.

Back on the Magellan, Panya hovered over her console as the altricion explored the floor in her immediate area. "Are you guys alright?" she inquired, relieved to at least hear a familiar voice even though it was Wade's.

"I should be asking you that," he answered. "What's happened?"

"A giant creature attacked the ship. It's still got us."

Aden suddenly interrupted. "Where are you now?"

"Captain, there have been some... developments," responded Wade tentatively. He knew his decision may not be popular with the rest of the crew, but his job was about getting things done and this was a matter of life and death. "I had to make an executive decision."

Aden drummed his fingers. Now what? He leaned into the comm. "Get to the point."

"I'm on my way back to the Magellan," he began. "I left Samara and the rest to deal with the situation at the Zumerian Sea." He stood by his decision and had no need to sugarcoat it.

"You *left them*?" Aden could not believe he was hearing this.

"It was the right decision," Wade replied, full of confidence.

"I want you to go *back*," commanded Aden.

"Sir, I'm already more than halfway back to the ship, and it seems to me that you could use my help." Wade knew precisely what to say to steer the captain toward agreement. He had done it for years. "The runabout's got the pulse cannons."

Aden considered this. It was true. The Magellan needed all the help it could get. If Wade could persuade this thing to either let go of the ship or roll over and die using the cannons, then they could pick up the others as they got the hell out of Dodge. "How soon until you get here?" he asked his XO.

"Before dusk," he said definitively. "Three hours tops."

This was likely enough time to do the necessary repairs. If so, the timing would be perfect. Hell, they could probably take off before the damned creature even knew what had hit it. "Alright. But we will do things my way from now on," he said. "Magellan out."

△△△

The ground shook as the land strider's massive foot connected with the harsh terrain. The ground team steadied themselves from the quake and continued toward its tail. Fortunately, the creature's lack of speed allowed them to close the final distance, with the tip of the tail towering over them a good ten feet. Still keeping pace with the strider, Samara called out to Takashi. "Get the Mech on the tail," she instructed. "It can help us up from there."

Takashi sped up to Mech and held onto its torso, trying to keep pace as the robot continued to jog effortlessly. "Meg, deploy your grapple," commanded Takashi. Without missing a beat or even changing its stride, Mech's right arm twisted and reconfigured. "Aim for the top ridge of the tail and fire," continued the Tech Officer. As Mech steadied its arm, Takashi grabbed hold of its body. The grappling hook shot out and slammed into the hide of the strider's tail.

As the metal cord tightened, Mech and Takashi were jerked off the ground and pulled up the side of the beast's tail. Takashi desperately clung on during the ascension, he wasn't the strongest person, and his muscles strained every second of the upward journey. He could endure the pain, the other alternative being plunging hundreds of feet to the ground. He gritted his teeth and weathered the pain.

Finally, they reached the end of the line a mere foot or so below the top ridge of the tail. Mech's accuracy never ceased to amaze the Tech Officer. Digging his feet into a pocket in the uneven and pocked skin of the creature, Takashi let go of Mech and quickly lifted himself onto the relatively flat top surface. A moment later, the robot joined him. It took a few seconds to get used to the movements of the creature. Fortunately, this was one area where its size was of benefit to the ground crew. Its slow and lumbering movement only caused a slight jostle from time to time once you were on its back.

Takashi gazed down at his remaining comrades on the surface, still managing to keep pace. They looked so tiny from this vantage point and in relation to the behemoth that had now become their ride. He turned to Mech. "Meg, stabilize your frame and lower the grapple to Samara."

Mech repositioned its body flat as its arms and legs reconfigured into something almost quadrupedal. A pair of smaller arms with small hooks at the end designed for mounting the droid for service or racking it up in the ship extended downward. They latched into the giant beast's flesh and then pulled themselves taught, locking the Mech in place. It reminded Takashi of the way the harpy lice of Sarn would latch onto their victims before sucking them dry of all vital liquid nutrients. He shook the thought from his mind — this was Meg, not a creature from Sarn.

Now secured, Meg lowered the grapple on its line. The

combination of the wind and the creature's movement caused the grapple to sway back and forth wildly. Takashi was concerned that the hook might become a deadly weapon that could brain or maim his crewmates, but he trusted Mech's abilities. She wouldn't let anything happen to Samara and Virgil. As the hook came mere inches from Samara's reach, Mech began to maneuver its arm in such a way as to immediately counter the movements around it. For a moment, it hung entirely still in the air directly within Samara's reach.

Breathing heavily from the exertion, Samara flailed her arms to grasp the dangling tether. Finally, she snagged it and hooked it to her belt. Grabbing hold, she was yanked off the ground. She yelled to Virgil. "Come on!"

Virgil turned and leaped up, throwing his arms around her. It was a messy collision, and he began to slip. "I'm gonna fall," he yelled with fright. With her free arm, she grabbed hold of the scruff of his collar and pulled him closer as they were hoisted upwards. As they moved skywards, he was able to climb up and reposition his body so they were pressed against each other face to face, arm in arm like lovers ascending toward the heavens.

As Samara fixated on the end of their journey upward, Virgil studied her face. She might be a stubborn pain in the ass, but she certainly *was* beautiful. Even up this close, her face was still mottled with dirt and grime. She was flawless. He wondered what it would be like to make love to a woman like her; she could probably show him a thing or two.

If there was one major negative to spending years as part of an elite survey team on a distant planet, the options for companionship were meager. It didn't help that most of his team was older, either. The Consortium was kind enough to supply ample amounts of Nalpimine to "whomever so desired." An ironic statement considering that Nalpimine pretty much wiped out all sense of desire altogether: saltpeter for the 22nd century.

He was honestly surprised that Gi-Dex didn't just covertly lace their water supply with it for efficiency's sake, though he wouldn't put it past them if they did.

Virgil's head was in his work, and he had his sister for companionship, and that was enough, or so he repeatedly tried to convince himself during his stay here. Being this close to a woman like Samara made him doubt many things that he once held true.

As the top rapidly approached, Samara looked down to see how high up they were and caught Virgil staring at her with an odd look on his face. He looked away, making the moment even more awkward. She smirked to herself. Boy, this guy was a piece of work.

They suddenly came to an abrupt stop, and Samara unhooked the grapple and stepped onto the strider as Mech disengaged its mounting hooks from the beast's flesh. What was left of the ground team huddled together as they assessed the current situation. "So far, so good," said Samara confidently. Turning toward the main mass of the strider, they readied themselves for what was inevitably coming next. The tail curved upwards hundreds of feet high, ending at the rear of its back. This was their destination. It was not going to be an easy climb.

"Last one to the top's buying," joked Takashi.

A moment later, their ascent began.

CHAPTER ELEVEN

Panya stroked the altricion in her arms as she stared out a portal in the main corridor at the massive slug-like beast that held them hostage. She wasn't scared anymore, so much as bored. It had been hours now since the first attack, and she thought that if it hadn't tried to kill them by now that it probably didn't plan to. This attitude left her with some free time to spend with her new little friend, and that had a way of calming her.

A door whooshed open as Oliver entered the corridor and walked by Panya. His face and hands were spattered with grease and oil. He regarded her with indifference. As much as he'd appreciate her help, he'd rather get the repairs done himself — that way he knew they were right and proper. She would probably just get in the way or ask a million questions anyway. He had decided that he'd just treat her cordially, especially considering that after they got off this insane planet, she was being kicked to the curb.

"Any new developments?" he asked, not expecting an answer. Panya just shook her head as Oliver continued down the corridor.

Resuming her visual exploration of the immediate area outside the porthole, a slight movement in the far distance suddenly caught her eye. "Wait," she called out to Oliver, now almost out of earshot. "I think I see something."

Oliver rushed over and peeked out another portal. Behind the giant slug, trees swayed in the forest as if something was headed toward the ship. "It's got to be Wade." He dreaded to think what the alternatives might be. "You'd better get to the bridge." Tucking the altricion into a makeshift sling made from two shirts hung from her shoulders, she nodded and headed down the corridor.

When she arrived at the bridge, Panya found Aden standing before the large viewscreen and in the midst of a heated discussion with Wade. "I don't like it," the captain said, frustrated by this new piece of business. "It's suicidal."

"Look, captain, I've got no intention of sacrificing myself," informed Wade. "So, if I didn't feel like this would work, I wouldn't suggest it."

Panya stayed toward the back as she tried to figure out what was going on. The conversation seemed deadly serious.

"Just make sure you can take off," Wade said as he signed off and the screen went black.

"Dammit!" cursed Aden at maximum volume.

"What's Wade going to do?" asked Panya.

Startled, Aden quickly turned to see Panya standing behind him. He thought he was alone on the bridge and would have preferred her to not see that outburst. The last thing he wanted was for his remaining crew to think he was cracking, which wouldn't have been so far from the truth. Aden rubbed his temples before answering. "He's hoping to piss it off enough to let go of us and come after him."

"That's crazy!" blurted out Panya. "Is he insane? What kind of plan is *that*?"

"Do you have any *better* suggestions?"

"We're all gonna die," she replied.

ΔΔΔ

Samara steadied her footing and stretched her arm higher as she traversed the surface of the tail, which jut from the creature's island-sized back at a moderate downward slope. To her left, Virgil was staying close. Takashi and Mech were high above, making better time. "Better pace yourself, Takashi," suggested Samara.

"Afraid I'm going to get to the top before you?" mocked Takashi. He knew Samara far too well. She always had to be first, always had to win in some way or another. Also, she was something of a bad sport.

"I'm just saying that we should stick together."

"You're just pissed that you're getting beat by a computer jockey." Takashi was enjoying himself. Very rarely did he find himself in a superior position to Samara, and he figured that he might as well take full advantage of it.

Two could play this game, so she attacked the only thing Takashi was sensitive about: the damned Mech. "It's not my fault that your girlfriend's got an unfair advantage," spat back Samara as she tried to quicken her pace.

"What? That I can turn off her speech when she starts whining?" Takashi laughed back at her. He saw right through her attempt to bait him.

Grabbing onto a chunk of coarse flesh, Samara repositioned her body and gave him the finger.

"That's what I thought," chuckled Takashi as he and Mech continued upward toward victory.

ΔΔΔ

The runabout slowly edged toward the feral slug and

stopped, holding its position a good hundred feet away. The giant creature remained stationary except for the rhythmic pulsing of its body against the ship's hull. Wade wondered if he was making a huge tactical mistake, but what other choice did he have? As far as he was concerned, it was past the point of no return, and better to push ahead with the plan, his plan, and hope for the best. He had made the decision. It was his duty to stick to it, no matter what the consequence. He only needed to look at the old burn scars on his hands to remind him of that. "I'm in position," he spoke into the comm. "You should have me on the monitor."

On the Magellan, Aden hurried down the hallway with Oliver in tow. "I want you to hold for my signal," he replied into his personal comm.

"Absolutely."

As they entered the bridge, Oliver took his position, and Aden plopped into the captain's chair. Panya maintained her console and brought up an exterior view as well as Wade on the sub-screen. They could make out the runabout in the distance behind the creature.

The image of Wade flickered briefly, then settled. "I'm going to leave the cockpit to man the pulse cannon," he told them.

"Go ahead," answered Aden before turning to his engineer. "Let's get the ship powered up."

Oliver attacked his console, double-checking switches and adjusting dials. They were going to get one chance at this, and it wasn't going to be his fault if it all went to hell. Out of the corner of his eye, Oliver saw on the monitor a tiny figure appear at the top of the truck and reposition the gun.

"We're powering up our engines now," Aden informed Wade. "Stand by."

"Ready whenever you are."

Aden turned to Oliver, who gave him a brief nod. It was time.

The Magellan trembled as the engines came online. The creature immediately began to stir. Its tail constricted a bit, tightening its grip on the hull.

Fully concentrated on the task at hand, Wade took a deep breath and steadied his aim. Sweat trickled down his face from where it was beading on his brow. This was his moment, his chance to be a hero, to redeem himself for all the past wrongs that people accused him of. This one act would wipe the slate clean. If only Samara and Takashi were here to witness this, then maybe they would think twice about mocking him behind his back or treating him like some kind of emotionless monster.

"Wade," Aden's voice interrupted his thoughts. "Fire at will."

Wade's sweaty hands gripped the pulse cannon controls as he depressed both triggers. Bolts of blue fire hurtled from the weapon and smacked into the side of the beast tearing a gooey hole in the soft tissue. The wounded slug convulsed as its mouths let loose a horrific screeching howl. As it twitched madly, another blast hit the creature, and it turned to seek out its attacker. Its massive head swayed, and its tail loosened its grip on the Magellan.

On the bridge, Aden, Oliver, and Panya were watching the action on the main screen. Brows were furrowed in concentration, faces expectant.

"I think it's working," surmised Panya. But this was based more on wishful thinking than any actual facts.

Aden enthusiastically yelled into the comm. "Wade. Keep it coming! It's starting to let go." He was glued to the monitor as a moment later his command was obeyed, and Wade fired another series of shots. The slug flailed around wildly each time it was hit, causing the Magellan to jerk and lurch with it. The ship was now sustaining damage from the sudden motions as much as the earlier attack.

Suddenly, the monster's head stopped and turned toward the runabout as one of the large transparent gelatinous sacs near the top of the creature parted and opened, oozing out a yellowish bile. Wade stopped firing to watch in amazement. Had he done it? Was this how these things die: oozing yellow goop? But before he could finish his thought, something surfaced in the center of the sac. Wade had to squint to focus on the form emerging from the slime.

It almost didn't register at first, as if his brain refused to believe. There it was: a human skeleton loosely wrapped in tattered clothes grappled from the skull by a chitinous, insect-like claw. It had a ring of hooks that appeared to hold onto the crown of the skull, and between them, he could see tendrils leading down into the cranium. The arm slowly unfolded as it reached the skeleton toward the runabout. The skeleton's eyes and the meat behind them were oddly intact, but the rest of its flesh had been stripped away as if digested by something. Its jaw hung open in what looked to Wade like a silent scream.

Momentarily mesmerized by the strange vision, Wade was caught off guard as a large mass of flesh pulsed and extended out from the center of the creature's elastic body and slammed full force into the vehicle like a battering ram. The truck was shoved into a nearby tree, knocking Wade forward into the cannon and out of his senses. Fortunately, the weight of the wheels kept the vehicle upright — the runabouts were designed to stay on their feet. As Wade looked around, he saw that the truck had sustained damage to its midsection, which was now crushed like a discarded soda can.

As the fleshy mound retracted seamlessly into the slug's body, the beast shifted its position closer to the damaged vehicle while continuing to hold out the corpse like a marionette. It swung it high above like some kind of organic periscope, turning it this way and that. Wade had the uncanny feeling that it was looking around through its eyes.

The crew of the Magellan watched in horror from the bridge. Leaning forward in his chair, Aden yelled at the screen. "Wade! Get the fuck outta there!"

Panya turned away, unable to look as the front section of the creature slowly crept closer and closer to Wade's position.

Within the wreckage of the runabout, Wade heard Aden screaming from his comm. "Run, Wade! Run!" Blood trickled down his forehead from the wound sustained by the first attack. Still dazed by the collision, Wade's head was swimming, and it was hard to focus. "Wade! Get the hell out of there!"

Whoever was yelling at him meant business. As he turned to look around for the source of the yelling, a massive shape appeared in his blurred vision. It was moving toward him, and his brain registered danger. Without another thought, Wade vaulted his body from the cannon position just as another fist of flesh hurled toward the runabout. The wrecking ball flesh of the creature crushed the truck against the tree, obliterating it into a mess of scrap metal.

Clear of the wreckage, Wade landed face-first on the ground. Entirely on autopilot, he got to his feet and ran toward the Magellan, giving the occupied slug a wide berth. As he ran, he caught a glimpse of the clothed skeleton hovering over the smashed truck as if studying the wreckage.

On the bridge, Aden surveyed the chaos unfolding before him. Even in their worst-case scenarios, they hadn't anticipated any of this. Not only was the creature on a rampage, but it also wasn't loosening its hold on them anymore. In fact, it had redoubled its efforts. The captain turned to Oliver, who furiously worked the controls.

"It's not letting go, captain," informed Oliver, who was showing signs of panic.

"Dammit!" yelled Aden furiously. He couldn't leave his friend out there to be pulverized by the creature. "Cut the engines and get the hanger open." Unbuckling himself, Aden thrust out a finger at Panya as he raced toward the exit. "Come with me." Panya had to scramble to catch up with him.

As Wade sprinted for the ship locked in the grip of the creature, the giant worm thrashed about and demolished the runabout behind him. Suddenly, the roar of the Magellan's engines silenced, and the transport vessel once again descended toward the surface on its landing thrusters.

Just before the landing gear touched the ground, the creature violently shook the ship to the right and smashed it against some large trees, breaching the hull. Inside, Aden and Panya were pitched around and smashed against the corridor walls. A moment later, the ship slammed on the ground near the landing pad. The force was so great that all the landing gear was either crumpled or snapped off as the vessel lay on its belly like a beached whale.

Aden got to his feet. "We have to get the bay door open now." Panya had only a moment to check that the altricion was still alive and in its sling before Aden snatched her up off the ground and pulled her through the now-wrecked corridor. It was filling with steam from the damaged return conduits that ran along its walls, and though the system would automatically shut them down there was no point in sustaining third-degree burns. They moved as quickly as they could through the damaged corridor.

His head now beginning to clear, Wade came to a sudden halt as he surveyed the nearly ruined Magellan lying in a heap and still in the clutches of the rear portion of the creature. It had all gone horribly wrong. Not only was the runabout destroyed, but his ship too, and probably the crew with it. Just about to give up all hope, the rear bay door of the Magellan began to open. A moment later, he could see Aden and Panya inside. Furiously, they motioned for him to hurry toward them. With renewed vigor, Wade sprinted toward safety.

Finished with its destruction of the runabout, the feral slug suddenly turned back toward the Magellan and focused the suspended skeletal remains toward the tiny figure racing to the back of the ship. Panya's anxiety heightened as the front section of the creature swiveled its face toward them and began slowly retracting its head into the rest of its body. Guided by the corpse, it would be on them within seconds.

"Wade! Oh God! It sees you," she screamed in terror.

Oliver exploded into the bay, joining the two at the lip of the open door. His eyes went to Wade, now closing the distance, but then traced upwards to the bizarre visage of the dangling skeleton moving toward his fleeing comrade from above. 'What the fuck is *that*?!"

As Wade sprinted for his life, a fist of flesh from the creature shot out and just barely missed the XO's back as it smashed a tree in the distance. The near miss caused Wade to stumble to the ground.

"Wade!" Without thinking, Oliver raced from the ship to his fallen comrade. As Aden was about to follow, Panya grabbed his arm. "No!!!"

Annoyed by the momentary delay, Aden shook her loose. "Let go of me!"

Oliver reached Wade in mere seconds. Thrusting out his hand to his friend, Wade grabbed hold just as another fist of flesh collided with Oliver, wrenching him from Wade's grip. In less than a second, Oliver's body was violently shoved across the field and squashed against a nearby tree. Just as quickly, the tendril retracted leaving a bloody mess of twitching pulp and crushed bone.

Panya screamed at the top of her lungs.

In sheer disbelief, Wade scrambled to his feet as Aden

closed the distance. The Slug moved toward them, and they both froze in place.

Aden whispered to Wade, "If we move, we're dead."

The captain was right, at least for the moment. The creature did not attack. Instead, it slowly extended the attached skeleton so it was hovering directly above the two of them. Manipulating it with its bony finger, like an eye on a stalk, the slug studied Aden and Wade with the human remains. Afraid to move a muscle, they allowed the examination to go on. As the slug emitted its strange howl, Aden considered the situation. They didn't have to die, not both of them, and it was the job of the captain to look out for his crew...

"Wade," spoke Aden calmly. "Tell Samara to stop living in the past and get on with her life."

Before Wade could process what Aden was saying, the captain turned and bolted away from the ship. The creature reacted instantaneously. It inexplicably released the skeleton from its grasp, which fell to the ground in a heap at Wade's feet. As the creature's now liberated insectoid appendage extended toward Aden, Wade made a break for the Magellan.

With his back to the action, Wade sprinted through the open bay door, leaving Panya the sole witness to the spectacle before her. "Oh god!" she cried deliriously.

As the captain ran toward the forest, a contented smile appeared on his face. This was a worthy sacrifice, and he was tired. This was *right*. It was time for something new.

A moment later, the feral slug's claw crashed down on his skull, knocking him to his knees. The appendages' skeletal fingers extended around the crown of his head and locked on. The tendrils inside hardened and drilled through his skull, burrowing into his brain. Aden winced in pain as tears streaked down his face. His final thought was of Samara. He hoped she would listen to him for once in her damned life.

As his body went slack, he was lifted off the ground. Flying through the air, it traveled via the arm as it was retracted into the gelatinous sac.

Within a second, Aden was gone.

$$\triangle\triangle\triangle$$

Samara stood at the top edge of the strider's carapace. From her point of view, it looked like the edge of a vast forest. It looked just like the surface of Vega, having dirt and trees that camouflaged the hard shell beneath. She turned to Virgil, who mapped out a scenario with Takashi and the Mech.

"It's just going to be a bit of a hike," Virgil informed them before turning his attention to Samara. "How are our supplies?"

"They'll hold until they pick us up," answered Samara confidently.

"That's rather optimistic considering we haven't been able to reach Wade or the Magellan for hours," reminded Takashi.

Samara turned to Takashi. "Yeah, brave new world," she said pensively. She then looked to Virgil, "Point the way."

CHAPTER TWELVE

Wade stood numbly in the claustrophobic shower stall as he washed off the dirt and muck that clung to his body. The water cascaded over a patchwork of scars and the coarse flesh of his chest and arms. Overwhelmed with grief, he gritted his teeth and banged the back of his head repeatedly against the plastic wall.

△△△

Her face red from crying, Panya curled in the corner of her quarters wrapped in blankets. The small silver packet of pills rested alone in a clearing on the floor in front of her.

The altricion wobbled up to it and pawed at the foil. She pushed the little creature away and reached for the packet. The universe was bleak and hostile. She had seen that. It had been shoved in her face. Was it any kind of place to raise a child?

△△△

As the team trudged through the forest, Samara fidgeted with her comm. "Ground team to Magellan," she spoke into it, desperate for a response. "Come in, Magellan."

"You just tried five minutes ago," reminded Takashi.

Stubborn as always, Samara ignored him. She refused to believe that her appeals were falling on deaf ears. "Magellan, this is the ground team. Come in."

Wade sat in Aden's chair alone on the damaged bridge of the Magellan, listening to her cries for help. "Magellan. Do you copy?" came Samara's voice yet again. Waiting for what seemed to be an eternity, Wade finally leaned forward and answered, "Go for Magellan," he answered, his voice devoid of any emotion.

Back on the land strider, a smile appeared on Samara's face. Takashi was a fool for not believing her. "Shit, Wade," she beamed into the comm, "We were beginning to think you left without us." She never thought she'd be happy to hear Wade's voice, but right now, she was ecstatic.

"What's your status?" Wade asked bluntly.

Samara was mystified by Wade's demeanor. "What's our status?" she asked incredulously. "We're fucked. That's our status."

"Samara, I need you to be serious." came the reply from Wade. It was as if they were discussing what supplies needed refreshing back at the dock instead of the life-threatening situation that they found themselves in. Wade had gone cold inside, becoming Wade Fassell the XO as opposed to Wade the person.

Samara was beside herself. What the hell was Wade's problem? This was so fucking typical of him. "Where's Aden?" she demanded to know. "I want to speak to him." At least Aden wouldn't act like a stuck-up prick.

There was a long pause.

"Wade, I said put Aden on the line!" Her patience was slipping again, but this time she was ready and willing for it to all flow out.

"He's busy," Wade said without skipping a beat, "assessing the damages." Even through her poor-quality personal comm,

Wade sounded unconvincing.

"Wade…"

"The runabout's destroyed," he said directly.

"What the hell's going on?"

"Have you made it to base camp?" asked Wade, avoiding the question.

"Not yet," Samara answered with irritation. "Now tell me what happened."

"The ship's been disabled," replied Wade. He calculated her most likely responses and decided it would be best to give her something to focus on to calm her down. "We need time to sort it out."

"Wade, we don't have enough food to hold out for much longer," said Samara with genuine concern.

"We're working on a plan."

"I thought the runabout *was* the plan— "

Virgil slammed his hand over the comm link. "We have less time than you think," he said ominously. "I've noticed changes in the air pressure…my ears popping. I think the strider's already reached the sea."

"Hold on a second, Wade," she said as she turned her attention to Virgil. "What are we talking about here?" she asked him.

"Unless you want to be pulled under as the strider submerges," he started dramatically, "a few hours, max." He released his hold of the comm-link.

She continued her conversation over the comm. "Wade, I don't know if you heard that, but you've got to get to us soon."

There was an exceptionally long pause. "Magellan out," came Wade's reply before the connection was severed.

Samara's hand dropped to her side. That wasn't exactly

the answer she wanted to hear. Something a little more definitive, like "We'll be there to pick you up within the hour," would have suited her better. Still, she knew Aden wouldn't abandon her; as soon as he got back to the bridge, he'd come to the rescue. He had always been good at coming to her rescue. She turned to the rest of the group, who stood looking on in silence and focused on Virgil.

"Come on, let's find your sister."

ΔΔΔ

Smashed and upended shacks encircled a central clearing that was once the center of the survey team's base camp. Busted-up treelike forms lay everywhere, testifying to the destructive force that ruined the once-peaceful research station. Virgil's heart began to hammer in his chest as soon as he saw the devastated camp that was once his home. This was the last place he saw his sister alive, but when he left a few weeks ago, the camp was intact and not the mess it was now. Something suddenly caught his attention in the debris. Dead bodies lay strewn around the wreckage, left for the elements or as food for foraging animals. One of the half-eaten bodies looked distinctly female.

Virgil immediately broke from the group and sprinted toward the encampment. "NARA! NARA!" he cried, his voice cracking in his throat as dread gripped him. He refused to believe that she was dead. Not like this. Not devoured by the very same creatures he dedicated his life to studying. As he closed the distance to the body, he secretly prayed that it was one of the others. Dr. Balasco was the same size as Nara but older. She had lived a good life, nearly 60 Earth years. Her death would be a noble sacrifice. Nara, however, would have been cut down well before her prime.

Samara, Takashi, and Mech maintained their normal pace as they watched Virgil race ahead. There was no point in running. Everyone was dead. It was obvious, even from their distant vantage point.

Takashi was the first to say what he and Samara were thinking. "What a fucking waste of time."

"Well, we're here, so we might as well make the best of it," she suggested, barely buying into her own words. "Ask Mech to scan the camp. Maybe we'll get lucky."

Feeling like this was an exercise in futility, Takeshi still gave the order. "Meg, scan for additional human life signs."

The robot paused for a moment as it processed the request. "One life sign detected, 71.3 meters, 12° North/West," informed the droid pointing in Virgil's general direction.

"That's Virgil, Meg," replied Takashi, a little annoyed. Meg should know better than to include Virgil in the search.

Takashi was even more shocked than Samara when Meg suddenly continued, "Life-form is human, female, height 5'2", weight unknown, condition unknown, signs of respiratory distress and elevated blood pressure present...."

Samara and Takashi felt like they'd been slapped in the face. Eyes now wide, they simultaneously bolted toward Virgil.

"Virgil! Wait!" shouted Samara as she ran.

Virgil either didn't hear her or chose to ignore her order. He kept his pace as he closed the distance to the female corpse sprawled out on a pile of debris. He stumbled and fell to the ground by the body. The sight was horrific, as was the smell, and it took all his will not to throw up as he picked himself off the ground and studied it. The woman's face was a mess of meat and skull. What was left of the hair was drenched in blood and gore. The mutilation was so severe that even Virgil, who had lived with these people, was unsure of the identity of the corpse. The mystery was solved when he brushed away a clump of matted hair obscuring the body's breast. The name on the jumpsuit confirmed his earlier speculation: this was Dr. Balasco, or at least what was left of her.

Samara's voice rang out behind him. "Mech's found a life sign," she said urgently, "but it's weak."

Virgil turned to her as she came to a quick stop in front of him. "It's Nara." He said with zero doubt in his voice.

"Don't get your hopes --"

"Where is she?" he demanded angrily, interrupting Samara.

Having just arrived, Takashi pointed to one of the still upright shacks nearby. "Meg says over there."

As Mech entered the open area in the center of the ring of shattered structures, the rest of them took off for the cabin marked SHACK-8. The edifice seemed structurally sound but had sustained quite a lot of damage, presumably from whatever creatures attacked the camp. Virgil paused momentarily at the door, inspecting the heavy scratches in the metal. "Please," he thought, "let Nara be in one piece." Sensing his anxiety, Samara put a hand on his shoulder. Shrugging it off, he shoved open the door.

The poorly lit interior mimicked the chaos outside: items were strewn everywhere, and furniture was toppled over. The place was a disaster.

"Nara?" Virgil called out for his sister, convinced she was the source of the life signs. "Nara, answer me if you can hear my voice," he said desperately. He pushed deeper into the mess inside the structure and began sifting through the rubble.

Meg appeared at the door, and Samara turned to it. "You wanna brighten this place up?"

"Unable to process request," replied the robot.

"Meg, use your lights to illuminate the room," Takashi

interjected to get the job done quickly. "Highlight the source of the life sign."

Mech panned the light through the darkness, stopping at a pile of junk in the far corner. The beam of the lights narrowed, focusing on one area, then widened again. Something in the pile shifted as the light hit it.

"Nara!" cried Virgil as he raced over and tore through the detritus. Within seconds, he found the survivor. Virgil dropped to his knees next to his younger sister, who lay in a daze amongst the ruins. She looked like she was in bad shape. Her short-cropped hair and wiry frame accentuated her spectral appearance.

"Virgil?" Nara said, straining to speak. Her eyes had trouble focusing and she appeared disoriented.

Virgil scooped her up in his arms and kissed her forehead. "Nara. I'm so sorry. Forgive me. Please forgive me," he begged her as tears flowed freely from his eyes.

"You came back..." she said with bewilderment.

Samara could see that the girl was severely traumatized and knelt next to them. She spoke calmly to Virgil so as not to upset him in his fragile state either. "You should let me examine her."

Samara was hoping he would simply relinquish his sister to her because the only other choice was to pry her from his arms. She decided to go to the source and appeal to Nara directly. "My name is Samara. I'm the Medical Officer from your supply ship, The Magellan," she introduced herself. "I want to take a look at you. Let's see where you're wounded."

"Okay," Nara answered simply. She then turned to her brother. "It's alright, Virgil," she assured him.

Virgil slowly released Nara and prepared to help Samara move her. Scanning the area behind her, Samara found what she was looking for. An overturned table lay within the wreckage.

"Takashi, get that table. I need a surface to work on." With Meg's help, Takashi got the table upright as she turned her attention back to her patient. "Anything I need to know about?"

"My arm…" informed Nara, "I think my right arm's broken."

"We'll be careful," she said as she took firm hold of the girl. "On two. One…Two…"

Samara and Virgil lifted Nara onto the makeshift examination table. She was a lot lighter than Samara was expecting, probably due to malnutrition and dehydration. The young girl hit the table with a whimper as she tried to fight through the pain. As Samara removed the medical instruments from Meg's internal kit, Virgil stayed close to Nara and wiped the sweat from her forehead.

"You were gone for so long," she started, "I thought…."

"I'm here now," he said, grief-stricken. Holding her left hand, he gently caressed her unkempt hair.

"They're all dead, Virgil," she told him. "All of them."

"I know."

Nara's eyes welled up. "I tried…"

He shushed her gently. She was starting to get worked up, and she needed to stay still as Samara ran her tests. Samara was just about finished with her bio-scan when he turned to her. "Well?"

"Other than the right arm, nothing physical," said Samara. "Just a bit dehydrated." Just as Samara initially thought.

Collecting herself, Nara turned to Samara. "The supplies ran out two days ago," she said. "I couldn't look for more. They kept coming back."

"Let's get some fluids in you and get your arm secured," she said to Nara. "This should hold you until we get you back to the ship." She opened another small compartment on Meg with a small red cross on it. Inside was an IV kit and a small unit of fluid for the mech to deploy in case it was needed during a rescue. It was part of a larger emergency medical kit housed throughout Meg's torso. She pulled the pieces out and assembled them, then connected the business end to Nara's wrist. Finally, she placed the setup back inside Mech and secured it in place.

Nara turned to her brother. "Are we going home now?"

Her question went unanswered as a sudden tremor rocked the ground, knocking the group around.

"What the hell was that?" asked Takashi.

Samara motioned to him and Virgil. "Go take a look," she ordered. "Mech and I will take care of Nara."

Takashi was first outside the door but waited for Virgil, who momentarily lingered at the entrance. Virgil's eyes locked with Nara's. She knew that look all too well, and it concerned her. "Virgil?" she asked hesitantly. "We are going home, aren't we?" Too ashamed to answer her, Virgil exited the building. "Let's take a look from up top," he said to Takashi as he made his way toward a lookout tower that loomed in the distance on the far end of the camp. The collapsible structure had sustained some minor damage but appeared to be stable. If he could get to the top, Virgil was convinced he would be able to get some answers about their status right away.

Takashi followed close behind, trying his best to ignore the human corpses that littered the area. Like the corpse of Dr. Balasco, the bodies were all mutilated in some way, and it was all too much for the young Tech Officer. He had never seen death up close before, and it profoundly disturbed him. He desperately tried to avoid the thought that this could somehow be his fate as well. The scenarios flitted through his brain like unwanted nightmares. He couldn't think of a worse fate than being eaten alive. Willing himself not to think about it, he refocused his mind on the task at hand. Having reached the structure, Virgil had already begun to scramble up the tower ladder. Takashi followed.

Climbing as fast as possible, Virgil scaled a hundred feet to the top with Takashi arriving shortly after. As he looked out at the expanse before him, all the color drained from his face. The situation was far worse than Virgil anticipated. From this vantage point, it was painfully clear that the land strider was more than half submerged in the Zumerian Sea already. The sea gel had already begun to creep up the back of the creature on all sides and slowly inched its way toward the base camp from all directions.

It was only a matter of time before it would overtake them, and they would either be sucked below with the creature or stranded on the surface of the gelatinous ocean far from shore, easy pickings for the creatures that lived just below the surface or those that scavenged from above.

Virgil turned to Takashi, "We've got to get off the strider right now, or we're all dead."

CHAPTER THIRTEEN

Sitting at Panya's console, Wade tapped away at the keyboard as the *Emergency Distress Beacon* banner flashed on the screen at the top of the monitor in front of him. He stopped typing as the computer requested the next piece of information: The number of personnel to be evacuated.

It was not as if he didn't know the response (he had been contemplating it for the last hour and had reached a decisive answer). It's that sometimes the thinking and the doing are at odds with one another. But as Wade was so good at, he had made peace with his decision, and he was not about to back down or alter his plan now. For better or for worse, that's not how he got to where he was in life. His finger found the number key and tapped it gently. The number "1" appeared on the screen. As the system posed the next question, the comm suddenly crackled with life, and a scratchy voice filled the bridge.

"Mayday! Mayday!" screamed Samara. Her desperation was palpable. "Come in, Magellan!" There was a long pause as she awaited a response. When one was not forthcoming, she continued her harried plea. "Aden, please reply. We need help!"

Wade continued to slowly tap out responses on the computer, ignoring the comm. He had already made up his mind. Samara and the others were already dead to him, and if this planet was going to take its sweet ass time getting it officially done, then so be it. He had more important things to take care of, and talking to the dead wasn't one of them.

"Aden! Mayday! Mayday!"

He tried to tune it out.

"Someone answer me!"

Wade gnashed his teeth and barked back at the comm without pressing the talk button. "I don't talk to ghosts," he informed no one but himself without even a trace of irony. As he reached for the volume control, another voice rang out.

"What are you doing?!"

It took Wade a moment to realize that the new voice was not emanating from the comm but directly behind him. Letting go of the knob, he whipped his head around to see Panya standing at the door with an unusual-looking creature cradled in her hands. Before he could explain himself, she raced for the nearest comm link, but Wade was faster. Out of the seat in seconds, he was on top of her before she even had a chance. He grappled onto her right hand and twisted it to gain control of her wild thrashing.

"Let go of me!" She screamed at the XO as she tried to break away, but at nearly half his size, she was no match for him physically, and all Panya could do was flail around, trying to squirm free. In the struggle, the altricion was knocked to the ground. Wade threw it a curious glance but had to turn his attention back to the crewmate who was giving him a run for his money.

"Hold still and listen!" He tried to order her.

"Magellan, come in!" came Samara again over the comm.

Samara's voice only fueled the fire in Panya. Deliriously, she continued to struggle against his hold. "Why don't you *answer them*?" she shrieked at her superior.

"And say *what*?!" he blurted out with a stern look in his eyes. "We can't help them!"

Upon hearing this revelation, Panya's exertions began to fade. "We've got to try *something*," she insisted.

"It's beyond our control!" he snapped as he shoved her to the floor.

"Please...," Panya begged, overwhelmed with emotion.

Samara's voice once again rang out, "Aden! Wade! Please help us! Magellan..."

Wade shut down the comm system before Samara could finish.

"You're insane!" screamed Panya, barely able to talk as she hyperventilated from the stress and exertion. Her mind raced. This couldn't be happening. Not like this. How could the crew's lives depend on someone as weak as she was? She was no hero, just a frightened little girl. One not even brave enough to handle her pregnancy, let alone save the lives of her new friends.

She looked up at Wade standing over her, lording over her much as her father did. Disgust built up inside her like bile rising to the surface. How dare he think that he could control her? That he could tell her what to do, how to behave. The hate was brewing. It was boiling over, and with it came a massive rush of adrenaline that overwhelmed her like a drug and gave her the courage she most desperately craved.

Without warning, Panya stood up and leaped at Wade, sending them both sailing across the room onto the bridge floor. She had summoned her inner rage, and it was spilling forth like an open faucet. "I hate you! I hate you!" she shrieked at him as she used her balled-up fists to assault him. She dug her sharp nails into his cheek and raked down the coarse flesh until she drew blood.

Wade spasmed as a jolt of pain hit his body. He suddenly countered with all his upper body strength, and Panya was easily tossed off and hurled against a console. Her head smacked against the metal surface, momentarily stunning her and immediately stopping her attack.

Now it was Wade's turn to lose it. Wiping the fresh blood

flowing from his face, he thrust an accusatory finger at the dazed girl. *"You* have no right to judge *me!"*

The altricion perked up at the loud noise and commotion and got to its feet. Locating Panya, it built up speed as it wobbled toward her. Unaware of the approaching creature below him, Wade continued his rant at the frightened girl who desperately wanted to flee but had nowhere to run.

"It's not my fault!" he cried as his eyes glazed over with madness. It sounded more like a plea for forgiveness than a statement of fact. His longing for redemption was made even more apparent to Panya when Wade's eyes dropped to glare down at his now bloodied hands to examine the old scars. "I couldn't put it out in time..." he sobbed. "I couldn't put it out...."

The altricion scurried into his view, drawing his attention away from his disfigured hands. He studied the bizarre-looking creature at his feet as it stopped and looked up at him. Wade was suddenly frightened. The fear twanged at his spine and infected his brain before bursting loose, "What the fuck is *that*?!"

Before Panya could scoop up the helpless creature, Wade pulled back his foot and booted the tiny altricion across the room. It smacked against the wall and tumbled to the ground. Panya screamed at the top of her lungs in horror. As the animal attempted to reposition itself, Wade rushed over and lifted his foot again, this time to squash it beneath his heavy boot.

Sensing immediate danger, the altricion's gills flared up and pulsated.

Wade cried out and reached for his ears as an unfathomable noise erupted inside his head. His foot came down clumsily next to the creature. The cacophony in his head was a typhoon of auditory stimuli that increased in volume by the second. The noise became a palpable heat that felt to Wade like his brain was being cooked in his skull. This was pain beyond pain. He continued screaming as his face turned bright red and his eyes bulged from their sockets.

Panya watched in confusion as Wade thrashed about. From her vantage point, she heard nothing except Wade's cries and the awful sucking sound of frothing spit collecting in his mouth and then splattering on the ground.

Wade's hands clamped to the sides of his head as if he was trying to keep it from exploding as he slumped to his knees. His eyes trained on the source of the phantom attack: the tiny creature now standing in a fixed position with arms outstretched and gills pulsating. It was closer now within reach. Desperate to stop the ear-piercing howl inside his head, Wade raised one of his fists high in the air. He meant to squash out the altricion's life. Smear its innards onto the bridge floor. Before he could complete the task, Panya scooped up her pet and raced out the door. The moment they were gone from the bridge, the altricion's howl ceased in Wade's head. Exhausted, he collapsed to the floor as drool poured from his mouth.

With the creature cradled in her arms, Panya bolted down the long corridor. Desperation wracked her face, "I'm so sorry. I'm so sorry," she sobbed as she stroked the tiny organism. "You're safe now. I promise. I won't let him hurt you." Panya's eyes scanned the scarred walls of the central corridor as she fled down the spine of the broken ship. She had no immediate plan other than to put as much space between her and the crazed XO as possible.

Back on the bridge, Wade's head began to clear, and as the final traces of the psychic assault faded away, a horrible realization washed over him. He once again examined his scarred hands. They were still balled into fists. Ever so slowly, the tension released, and his fingers fanned out. Sanity slowly seeped back in. *What am I doing?* he thought as he contemplated his actions. He was out of control and unable to stop himself. Was he capable of hurting her? Had it come to this?

A red indicator light flashed on the control panel before him. Wade glanced at it as his eyes went wide. Someone had opened the main hatch. There was only one person it could be. "Panya," he said as he scrambled to his feet and raced out the door. Wade's mind swam. What was she thinking? The only thing that lay beyond the main hatch was certain death. He quickened his pace down the central corridor, praying as he ran that he wasn't too late. As he got closer to the main junction, he called out to her. "Panya!" He turned the corner to find her at the mouth of the hatch. The entrance was wide open. "Stop!" he implored the young girl.

Behind her, the massive shape of the feral slug loomed quietly. "Stay back!" she hollered at the XO. "Don't come any closer!" She warned him as she stepped toward the exit to demonstrate her seriousness.

"Panya, you need to shut that door *right now*," he said sternly. This was no time to screw around. The slug was beginning to stir, and it could be a matter of seconds before it chose to attack. With the main hatch open, they were completely vulnerable. Given the flexibility of the creature's body, there was no telling what havoc it could wreak if it could breach the ship's interior.

"I won't let you hurt him," cried Panya, referring to the altricion in her hands.

Arms outstretched, he beckoned her toward him. "I'm not the one you have to worry about." He lowered his voice and continued to her calmly. "Now, please close the hatch, and we'll discuss this rationally." He took a step closer.

Without warning, Panya pivoted on her heels and raced out of the exit.

"No!" screamed Wade incredulously.

Panya sprinted onto the surface of Vega Prime but only got a few hundred feet when something dropped into view directly in front of her blocking her escape. It took a second for the true horror of the moment to grasp Panya as she stood face-to-face with her former captain. Suspended by the chitinous arm of the feral slug, Aden Harker hovered above the ground eye-to-eye with her. His blank stare looked straight through her, and his entire body was covered in a viscous substance teeming with microscopic life.

Panya screamed at the top of her lungs as the world melted into blackness.

CHAPTER FOURTEEN

"Come in Magellan! We need help!" Samara yelled into her comm, frantically pleading to be heard. There was no reply after over ten minutes of trying.

Takashi put his hand on her shoulder. "They're not coming for us."

She flung her comm unit at a nearby rock, shattering it to pieces. Letting her arm drop to her side, Samara peered out at the forest. For the first time in a while, there was a crack in her demeanor. She looked lost and frightened, more like the scared teenager that Aden found in the ruins on that day. She felt helpless, and all she wanted to do was curl up in a ball and die as she let the alien sea sweep her away into oblivion. Samara turned her head to the others and watched as Virgil finished bandaging Nara's right arm. At least those two have each other, she thought. They won't die alone away from their loved one like she would.

The moist sound of the thick gel rapidly approached. As the noise began to envelop the area, something inside Samara shifted. She could feel something of her old stubbornness, and it was bubbling back to the surface. It nipped at her mind and told her not to give up. It convinced her that she wanted to live and should *refuse* to lie down and die.

The idea surged from her mind to her body, amping her up and making her angry. How could she have even contemplated giving up? It wasn't an option. She looked at the downtrodden faces of the others, suddenly thinking how foolish they were to think this was the end. "We're not going to die like this," she said firmly and with authority. "Do you hear me?" She crossed to Virgil and grasped him firmly by the shoulders. "Think, Virgil,' she demanded. "You're the one who knows this place."

Virgil scanned the immediate area but drew a blank. "I--"

"Come on, Virgil," she pressured him. "There's got to be something here. Something that flies or floats--"

Nara suddenly sprung to life. "The skiff!" she proclaimed.

"What?" asked Samara.

"The skiff!" the younger girl repeated. "It's what we call the all-terrain vehicle we use to pick up your supplies with," she added as clarification.

Takashi was far from won over by this revelation. "What good will that do us on the water?" he asked.

"The Zumerian Sea is not water," she said gleefully, pleased with herself. "It's a gelatinous organism."

The others just stared at her blankly. They did not get her meaning at all.

"The skiff will float," she said exuberantly. "It will float, and the treads of its tires are designed to pull it across bodies of liquid. There's more to the mechanics of it, but you get the idea."

That was all they needed to hear. Within minutes the entire group was down at the foot of the camp searching for the "skiff" amongst the ruins. Samara was the one who found it buried beneath a clump of dead vegetation. "Over here!" she cried out. They hurried over to help clear the debris and reveal the bottom wheels of the all-terrain vehicle. "Help me turn it over," she instructed as she moved to the side of the upturned frame and dug in her shoulder. Fortunately, the skiff was lightweight, having been made of poly-plastics and low-density metals. It only took a coordinated shove from Samara, Virgil, and Takashi to get it upright.

Nara, still attached to Mech via the IV, watched as

they inspected the vehicle for damage. The tiny truck had a square-shaped rear end lined with benches designed to hold a small contingent of people. The six chunky wheels rested on separate axles, and a single large engine positioned at the rear provided impressive amounts of power. Everything appeared to be in good order. These machines were built to last this one apparently had. Still, there was only one way to be sure.

Virgil hopped into the single-chaired cockpit at the front of the vehicle and said a quick prayer before depressing the starter. The engine revved with life. "She's working," he sighed with relief.

"Alright. Let's pile in," suggested Takashi, ready to get the hell out of Dodge.

Nara interjected before they had a chance to comply. "We need to find some rope or cable."

"She's right," agreed her brother, surprised that he didn't think of it himself. "We have to be able to attach ourselves to the skiff somehow in case we get knocked overboard."

"Lifelines?" asked Samara.

"Yeah," began Nara having everyone's undivided attention. "The sea is like...gelatin. Our bodies aren't exactly designed to move in it." She had a good point. If any of them fell overboard, it could and likely would be a disaster. Better to be safe than sorry. They were only going to get one chance at survival.

"Go help Mech with Nara," Samara instructed Takashi. "Virgil and I will take care of the lines." As everyone set about their tasks, the sound of impending doom advanced.

△△△

Panya's eyes fluttered open, and she found herself lying

down in the sick bay. Still dazed, it took her a good minute to regain full consciousness. As she turned to her right, she saw Wade standing by the door. Her mind raced as synapses fired in her brain warning her of danger. She instinctively cringed away as he slowly moved toward her.

"Shhh...shhh...It's okay," he said in a soothing voice. Panya wasn't sure what his intentions were, and she scanned the room for a means of escape. "Everything's alright," continued Wade. "You're safe."

"What's... what happened?" asked Panya, still frightfully confused.

"You fainted," he informed her as he pushed a nearby button, and a small platform extended from the wall. Sitting down on it close to her, he dropped his head in shame. "Panya... I let my past catch up with me and push me over the edge," he stammered, deeply embarrassed. As he rubbed his eyes, she looked at his scarred hands.

"Where's... my pet?" she insisted, still not convinced of Wade's sincerity.

"It's unharmed," he responded awkwardly. "I... Well, it's outside. With Aden."

"Aden!" The mention of his name caused all her more recent memories to flood her brain. She had seen the captain alive. He stood directly in front of her. But, no, there was something off about him. He looked dead, soulless. That's right, she thought -- those soulless eyes. That's what made her scream. Made her disconnect and tumble into the void. They scared the hell out of her.

As the wheels turned in Panya's head, Wade continued his observation of events, "I think it's communicating with him."

Panya suddenly felt centered as she turned to lock her eyes with Wade. "I want to see," she demanded.

Wade nodded his head.

$$\triangle\triangle\triangle$$

The main hatch opened before Wade and Panya. In front of them, the slug beast rested calmly as Aden knelt on the ground. He was held in place by the arm that extended from the Slug's body. The former captain of the Magellan had a vacant stare on his glistening face and paid no attention to the new spectators. His arm was stretched to the ground before him with the altricion latched onto his wrist. The tiny creature's gills throbbed and flexed rhythmically.

"They've been like this for over an hour now," Wade informed her.

"And the others?" she asked tentatively.

"I think it's just us now," he answered stoically.

Panya didn't protest this time. This was the response she had expected. Her new friends were dead, and no amount of fretting over it was going to bring them back. Better to just accept the truth and move on.

$$\triangle\triangle\triangle$$

The skiff was ready to go. Nara and Mech were loaded inside first as Takashi helped to situate them in the back of the vehicle. "Meg, listen," he instructed the robot. "You must hold onto Nara at all costs. Whatever happens, do not release her until we are safely on land." The Droid's arms pulled the young girl gently into its embrace. It knew the exact amount of pressure to apply to hold her safe but not cause her any discomfort. "I suggest you latch yourself to the vehicle too," continued Takashi as hooks on Mech's torso like the ones it used on the strider's back emerged from its rear. They dug into the metal hull and secured it and Nara to the interior. Takashi gave the two of them a quick once over. "Are you comfortable?" he asked Nara.

"Yeah," she answered with a bemused look on her face. "She's remarkably gentle for a Mech."

Takashi beamed with pride. Whether Nara knew it or not, her surprise was a compliment to the months of work he had spent fine-tuning and tweaking the robot, and this was the first time someone took any notice. He smiled at her. "Meg...I call her Meg."

Nara smiled back. "That's a pretty name."

A hint of red washed over Takashi's face, and he turned away before she could see the telltale signs of embarrassment. He instantly recognized the feeling in his belly. It was the butterflies that told him that he liked this woman and maybe even found her physically attractive. He unfortunately never had much luck with this sort of thing, so he had become shy in nature. It was even worse with the girls that he fancied — his heart fluttered, his belly fluttered, and his thoughts fluttered into a jumble. Fortunately, having Panya onboard had given him some practice in interacting with ladies.

The Comms Officer wasn't his type, so he saw her as more of a sister than a prospective mate. She saw him as non-threatening and treated him as a friend and confidant. Their friendship worked well. Nara was something altogether different. She was his type, and he suddenly became self-conscious as he took his seat next to the others. Takashi thought about the irony of finally meeting a pretty girl that he had a chance with in the middle of a life-and-death situation on an alien planet located on the outskirts of the known universe. "This will be one for the grandchildren," he thought optimistically.

Samara handed each of the remaining passengers thin

cables that were hooked onto the perimeter around the bed of the skiff at various points. "Wrap them around your waist and secure them with these," she insisted, holding out some metal clips to them. As instructed, everyone went about the task. The sooner they got it done, the sooner they could get off the submerging beast and to the safety of the ever-retreating shoreline.

Virgil suddenly let his tether fall to the ground as he leaped up from his seat and crossed to his sister. He had a wild-eyed look that instantly scared Nara. "The data deck," he said, keeping his voice low.

"The zephyrs tore this place apart," she answered in a hushed tone, concerned that he was about to do something stupid. Neither of them appeared to want to share this with the group. This was between the two of them.

"Did you even look?" he demanded.

Samara had no idea what Virgil was discussing with his sister, but she was in charge, and the only thing he should be concerned with at this moment was getting the cable secured around his mid-section so they could get away. "Virgil, get your tether on," she ordered, quite annoyed. "We have to leave." This was no time for a family chat.

Focused solely on his sister, Virgil chose to ignore her. "Years of work, Nara." he reminded Nara as she hung her head to avoid his eyes. She knew in her heart that Virgil was right. The data deck was everything. It was the primary backup of all their years of research. Without it, all their work -- all their blood, sweat, and tears were gone forever. The death of the other team members would be for nothing. Almost imperceptibly, Nara's head nodded up and down. That was all Virgil needed to see. He whispered something into Nara's ear and then flew over the side of the vehicle, landing with a thud on the ground.

Samara was livid. "Get in the skiff!"

"I'm not leaving without it," informed Virgil with a determined look in his eyes. Before Samara could reply, he bolted back to the camp.

Samara turned to Nara. "Leave without what?" Nara kept tight-lipped, which only pissed off Samara more. "Where the hell is he going?"

"He'll meet us at the hill," said Nara pointing to a raised area nearby. In the distance beyond the hill came the sound of snapping trees and the panicky howls of drowning creatures.

"Idiot!" shouted Samara as she watched Virgil disappear behind one of the remaining shacks. Having no other choice, she dropped into the driver's seat and accelerated the skiff as they drove off away from the doomed last remnants of the survey camp.

△△△

Panya sat on the ledge of the main bay door watching the activity of the indigenous creatures. The altricion continued to hold onto Aden's hand as its gills pulsated rhythmically. They had been like this for hours. The lack of activity was starting to take its toll on Panya. It's a fantastic thing about the human condition that a thing that could be so wondrous and alien could soon become tedious and tiresome. All it takes is the right amount of time.

As she started to yawn, something new happened, and her jaw quickly snapped shut. Afraid to even move, lest she accidentally distract the participants, she observed in complete silence as the altricion released Aden's hand and turned to her. Panya almost forgot to breathe as the tiny creature wobbled closer. Ever so slowly, she rose from the stoop and stepped forward to meet it. Gently, she reached down and picked her little friend up. Having taken her eyes off the captain and the feral slug for a few moments, she was surprised to see a sudden movement out of the corner of her eye.

Aden's body was hoisted off the ground and shoved close to her. Before she could retreat, he stopped and hung before her at a comfortable distance. Nervously, Panya studied the corpse. Even though he was, for all practical purposes, dead, his face didn't look like it. The expression he wore was not the slackness of death but one of sadness, or at least this is how the overly sensitive Comms Officer read it. It deeply moved her. She just as sincerely hoped that he wasn't suffering.

"I'm sorry, captain," she said quietly. She was pretty sure he couldn't hear her, but she still felt the sentiments were worth expressing.

She was not even slightly prepared when Aden's mouth began to move.

Panya was aghast as she watched his lips try to form words. A breathless noise expelled from his lungs as if the corpse was unaware of even the basic mechanics of speech. She continued to stare at him as he struggled with the rudimentary act when it occurred to her what words he was trying to form. They were her own being repeated back to her: "I'm sorry, captain."

The simple expression horrified her. As she put her hand to her mouth, Aden silently mimicked her movement with his hand. All at once she realized what was going on, and it made her feel lightheaded. She was communicating.

Renewed with wonder, Panya moved in a little closer. "Captain," she said tentatively, "Can you understand what I'm saying?"

He didn't mimic her this time. Instead, his face contorted as if he was trying to process some very complex information.

He then mouthed a series of words. This was not a rerun of her question; it was an actual reply. Panya couldn't immediately figure it out. She moved a step forward as he repeated it once more. This time, she could perceive a barely audible sound: a whispered breath.

"Can you speak?" she asked inquisitively.

His face registered sadness and frustration as he continued to mouth the inaudible words. Now only a foot away, Panya ever so slowly pressed her ear close to his mouth. If this were a ploy to bring her in close for the kill, she wouldn't have a chance and she knew it. She didn't care. Something inside assured her that the captain's motives were on the level and that she wouldn't come to any harm. Reason would suggest that she was being foolish, considering that a team of experienced scientists exploring this planet had been almost entirely wiped out because they second-guessed what the creatures here were capable of. Panya didn't go for science; she was led by her heart and emotions — and right now, they told her to listen to the captain. As she closed her eyes and strained to listen with her ear mere centimeters from his reanimated lips, she heard something that made her eyes go wide.

"I need Samara...."

CHAPTER FIFTEEN

The colossal land strider sunk deeper and deeper into the Great Sea. A mile out from the land, its body was almost entirely submerged.

High above, a pack of drifters passed by casting shadows upon the ground team huddled in the skiff atop a small hill. Below them, the turquoise gel water rose at a steady pace. It was only a matter of time. Samara scanned the slowly disappearing valley below for any sign of Virgil.

"Do you see him?" asked Nara, concerned for her brother's safety.

"He's going to get us all killed," replied Samara, annoyed by the situation they now found themselves in. If it wasn't one thing, it was another.

△△△

The door to Shack 2 creaked open, and Virgil entered the dilapidated construct. The interior was even worse than Shack 8, where they found his sister. He immediately crossed to the room's far end and a wall unit that had been left unlocked. He ripped open one of the cabinets but found the cubby empty. "Shit," he said to himself. "Can't anything be easy?" His eyes quickly shifted to the debris on the floor as he scanned the immediate area. As luck would have it, he immediately found what he was looking for. Jutting out from the mess was the corner of a worn silver case about the size of a portable computer. It was the data deck wedged under a collapsed table. Racing to it, he grabbed hold and yanked, but it wouldn't budge.

"Virgil! Get back to the skiff!" came Samara's barely audible voice from somewhere outside in the distance.

Ignoring the request, he squatted down low and positioned his legs against the table edge for leverage. Once again, he tugged at the case. Slowly, it started to give until it unexpectedly came loose, knocking him backward and onto the ground. As he rose, he discovered the reason for the struggle: A human hand clutched the silver case's handle. Just as the shock wore off from seeing the lifeless appendage, it suddenly twitched and jerked backward, taking the case with it. "Oh my God!" screamed Virgil as he scrambled over to the arm. "Hey. It's Virgil!" he yelled to the pile of debris entombing the survivor, "Can you speak?" Virgil waited for a reply but got only silence followed by some rustling within. "I'm going to get you out of there," he instructed. "Just hang tight."

Virgil's mind raced. He wondered who it could be. It was a man's hand, so that ruled out some of the team. Could it be Terry? Terry was his only other close friend next to his sister. They had bonded early on and became fast friends. It would be a miracle if it were him. Virgil grabbed hold of the table and lifted it with all his might but only managed to raise it a mere two inches because it was weighed down by fallen debris. His arms ached as he continued to lift. Virgil was determined to rescue whoever it was, and the searing throb of muscle pain would not stop him. Still straining to lift, he peered into the gap to check for signs of life. It was dark within the rubble, and almost impossible to make out any features. "Can you move at all?" he said as he struggled to keep the table aloft. In the blackness, there was some movement. "Can you hear me? I'm going to need your help." He lowered his head slightly as his eyes adjusted to the dark.

Without warning, a snake-like creature with a wide mouth and rows of sharp teeth lunged at him. He instinctively released the table and sprawled backward, barely escaping its bite. The heavy metal table slammed down on the creature's head, crushing it into the hard ground. As Virgil scrambled back to his feet, he tried to make sense of what had just happened.

Unfortunately, he only had a moment to think as a loud creaking suddenly filled the small space, and sea gel began to seep into the room. Panicking, Virgil grasped the dead hand holding the data deck and pried open fingers that were tight with some form of rigor. The person was quite dead, probably devoured by the creature that nearly got Virgil. Maybe it was for the best that he never discovered the man's identity. It was no way to die, especially for someone as likable as Terry.

The sea gel lapped up against Virgil's pants as he tugged on the case. He finally pulled it loose just as the way he had come in suddenly became impassable. He needed to find another exit, and the only way was up. He checked the ceiling and located a hole probably caused by the earlier destruction of the camp. It was accessible by utilizing the junk piled below it. Scrambling upwards, the sea rapidly rose around him.

Samara, Takashi, and Nara watched as the gel enveloped the remains of the base camp. Afraid to look into Nara's eyes, Takashi turned to Samara. She shook her head. As far as she knew, Virgil had paid the ultimate price for his foolishness. "It should be any minute now," Samara informed the others.

A shrill bark behind them grabbed their attention. On the peak of a faraway hill, a grayish, humpbacked quadruped scurried about in a frenzy, trying to stay alive above the sea. This only prolonged the inevitable. The creature was doomed.

Samara watched unemotionally as the beast was swallowed up by the viscous ocean. "This place is a nightmare...."

"I see him!" screamed Nara as she wiggled around in

Mech's grasp. All eyes turned to where the young scientist was pointing. In the distance, Virgil raced across the roof of Shack 2 carrying the data deck and made his way toward a high tree that leaned against the structure. "He's trying to get to higher ground," she remarked anxiously. "Hang on!" she yelled to her brother at the top of her lungs. "We'll come and get you!"

As Virgil arrived at the tree, he turned and acknowledged his comrades. "You'd better hurry!" he yelled back. Not a second later, the sea gel overtook the roof. Virgil scrambled up the tree, which was made even more awkward by the heavy case he was transporting.

A moment later, the skiff rocked slightly and was lifted upwards by the gel. "Alright, hold on," reminded Samara as she fired up the engine and put it in gear. The vehicle's broad bottom floated upon the surface of the sea just as Nara had promised them it would. The dense nature of the sea allowed for smooth navigation as the skiff slowly trundled along, dragged by its half-submerged wheels with their deep pockets and retractable flaps. They were making good time as they approached the tree that had become Virgil's last-ditch hope for survival. He smiled as they got closer and readied himself to jump.

"Got room for one more?" he joked as the skiff positioned itself directly underneath him.

"Just get in the goddamn truck," yelled Samara. Just because everything worked out did not mean that he hadn't put everyone's lives in danger. She was still pissed.

He dropped the silver case into the back, and it landed with a thud by Mech's feet. He then dangled himself from a sturdy branch and dropped down to the awaiting skiff. He conked his head against the side rail as he sprawled into the back, but that was a minor price to pay. Wincing at the pain, he still managed to crack a smile at his sister. "I got it," he said, referring to the data deck lying at her feet.

"I hope that was worth almost dying for," said Samara,

still irritated by the unwarranted adventure.

Virgil was beyond caring about what Samara thought. He knew it was worth it from the look of pride in Nara's eyes.

A loud sucking sound drew everyone's attention, and they all turned to watch the last of the land strider disappear into the murky depths of the Zumerian sea. "Amazing," said Virgil, awestruck by the spectacle. It was a magnificent sight, and the majesty of it was not lost on any of them. They had just witnessed something no human eyes had seen before, and they all hoped that they'd live long enough to recount the tale.

Takashi saw something floating toward the surface and fixed his attention on it. The object was one of the dead bodies of the survey team. He motioned toward the female corpse as it was dragged back down below. "At least she'll get a proper burial at sea," he said somberly. Turning toward the shoreline, which seemed so very far away, he pondered what fate had in store for him and the others.

△△△

Wade sat on his bed holding a photograph in his scarred hands. He stared at it intensely as his mind wandered off into the dark corners and quiet recesses of his memories. Fifteen years past seemed like a lifetime ago, but the memories were still as sharp as they ever were. They still stung. Wade could easily summon up the sirens blaring in his ears that pierced his skull or re-experience the burning steam and smoke that had filled up his lungs every time he took a breath in the Magellan's central corridor. Now, at this moment, he felt all of it, and it all knitted together into something more solid, more of a waking dream than a mere memory.

Wade's face dripped with sweat as a younger version of himself was reborn from the memories that traced their way through his head. A version of him that was the captain of the Magellan and responsible for the lives of everyone on board.

ΔΔΔ

Wearing disheveled clothes, the younger Wade paced frantically by a sealed metal door as Oliver raced to him and grabbed him violently by the collar. "Why did you seal the hatches?!" he shouted incredulously at his superior.

"The ship's going to blow," replied Wade authoritatively.

Muffled screams and cries for help emanated from beyond the locked door, sending Oliver over the roof with anger. "*If you vent, they'll all die!*" he screamed.

Wade pushed Oliver off of him and lunged for the door's manual override. The metal handle instantaneously seared his flesh, forcing Wade to think through his sudden change of plans. Oliver was right – they had to unseal at least this hatch to save the remaining crew. Tearing off his shirt, Wade quickly wrapped it around the handle. "Give me a hand," he barked at the burly engineer. The two men struggled to turn the handle, but the progress was slow going. As the door slid open a sliver, hands reached through the small opening. "Help us!" desperately cried one of the crew beyond the door as his hands clawed at the men.

Aden and a youthful Samara appeared at the far end of the long central hallway, confused by the commotion at the other end. They raced over to Oliver and Captain Fassell. "What's happening?" Aden yelled out to Oliver, straining to be heard over the loud warning sirens.

"The captain sealed off the rear section to try to contain a hull breach," Oliver explained quickly.

"How many of the crew are back there?" asked Aden frantically.

"Four. Fisher, Reyburn, Teller, and Bates," answered Oliver, still straining with the handle.

"If I didn't seal it, we'd all be dead," explained Wade, attempting to justify his decision. "It bought us some time to equalize pressure levels and start looking at ways to hold the ship together."

Grabbing hold of the manual override handle, Aden joined the others in trying to open the door to the aft section.

"Aden!" cried out Teller from beyond the door, "Don't let us die!"

Aden turned to Samara, who was watching the scene unfold from a few feet away. Her eyes were filled with fear as the screaming from beyond escalated. "Samara," he called out to her, "Get back to the bridge," he instructed. She was near catatonic, frozen with horror. "Samara!" he screamed. "Listen to me. I need you back on the bridge! *Samara! NOW!*" His words finally sunk in, and she turned her attention from the men on the other side of the door to her mentor.

"But..."

"Get the hell out of here!" Aden screamed at her.

Absolutely terrified, Samara sprinted back down the corridor toward the bridge, but unknown to the others, she stopped at the far end and hid behind a large conduit to watch the drama unfold. Aden and the others continued to struggle with the handle, but the door wouldn't move any farther. The intense heat had caused the door to fuse with its seals, making it almost impossible to open, even with the three most muscular men on the ship wrenching it with all their collective strength.

"We've got to get my men out of there," yelled Wade. "That's an order!"

Oliver and Aden looked at one another. This was not an order they could fulfill. Oliver looked at a nearby display panel, and it became plain that there was only one choice. "Captain, we've reached critical levels of fire and off-gassing," informed Oliver as he let go of the manual override, "We've got to vent now."

Wade couldn't believe he was hearing this. "I won't give that order," he snarled.

"Then we'll lose the whole ship!" informed Aden, also releasing his hold on the handle.

Wade didn't want to hear any of this, and his mind tried to avoid the inevitable truth, but the decision had to be made. The order had to be given. He turned toward the men only a few feet from him, trapped on the other side. They were desperate to live. Slowly, Wade's grip loosened on the handle. "I'm sorry...." He said to no one in particular.

A massive explosion erupted from behind the door, and a wall of flame shot outward, blasting into Wade, and knocking him to the ground in a flaming heap. Using their jackets, Oliver and Aden smothered out the flames on their captain as quickly as they could. They peeled off the fabric that wasn't stuck to him to discover Wade burned over most of his body. The captain was in desperate need of medical attention. "I'm sorry," he wept pathetically as he looked up at Aden.

"Captain," said Aden gravely, "you have to give the order."

There was a long silence. Wade nodded slightly. "Do it..." he said weakly before succumbing to the horrendous pain that ravaged his body and passing out.

As Aden turned, he discovered Samara right behind him, looking on in shock. He pulled her close to block her view as Oliver spoke into the ship's comm, "Fletcher, this is a direct order from the captain," he said without emotion, "Vent the rear section immediately." Oliver pressed a button on the door console releasing the manual override, and the door slammed shut. A moment later, the hull vibrated as the air was sucked from the rear section averting the crisis and destroying any hope that the crew behind it had survived.

$$\triangle\triangle\triangle$$

Wade's comm-link crackled with static, jarring him back to the present. He rubbed his scarred face as a male voice filled his quarters.

"Come in, NTSS Magellan," said the voice. "This is the URS Paladin. We have received your distress beacon. Over."

Dropping the photo to the bed, Wade responded to the call.

"This is the Magellan. We read you, Paladin," he said calmly.

"Roger. We are en route and should be at Vega Prime in about one day. Will you be needing medical assistance?"

"Negative, Paladin," replied Wade, "just a shuttle transport."

"Copy, Magellan. Paladin out."

As Wade got up, the photograph he was looking at slipped off the bed and drifted to the floor. Wade reached down to retrieve it and studied it a moment longer. The picture was of a group of ten rough and tumble kind of guys collected in front of a much newer-looking NTSS Magellan. A younger Wade stood at the center, smiling proudly. Kneeling next to him was Aden, a youthful Samara, and a smirking Oliver Tross. The edges of the photo were slightly singed.

CHAPTER SIXTEEN

Samara dipped her hand into the Zumerian Sea and let the gel collect up to her wrist. It was an odd sensation. The gel was warmer than she expected, and though it had the feel of something like gelatin, it didn't behave like it. The viscous fluid had life and purpose, and as she lifted her hand and studied the stuff, it shifted around and slid off to join the rest of the ocean once again. Curiously, she turned to Nara for an explanation, "So what is this stuff?"

"It's an organism, for lack of a better word," answered Nara, pleased to talk about something she was passionate about. "For the longest time, we thought it was like our oceans on Earth, but we soon discovered that it possessed rudimentary intelligence. That's why it was so eager to rejoin its body," she added, referring to the gel that Samara scooped up. "Other than that, we don't know much about what makes it tick because it's like a sentient element that, in one way, is a crucial component of Prime's ecology and, in another way, completely autonomous. The oddest aspect of the Zumerian Sea is that it's comprised mostly of Oxygen. You can breathe it."

"Are you *serious*?" asked Takashi, surprised by this revelation.

"It's true," confirmed Virgil. "You can't drown in it."

"You can't drown?" questioned Takashi incredulously.

"That's right," confirmed Nara.

As Takashi placed his hand in the organism, a series of

dark elongated fins rose from the depths and passed by the skiff. He instantly withdrew his arm. "What the hell was that?"

"It looked like a ray cutter," postulated Nara. "There are creatures that live within the sea. Sort of symbiotic. Like the land strider, the ray cutters need the Zumerian organism to procreate.

"Great," said Takashi sarcastically. "Well, I want to procreate someday myself. So, let's just concentrate on getting to the shore in one piece."

Nara smiled at Takashi. She found his anxiety amusing and opened her mouth to speak. She was suddenly interrupted as something slammed into the skiff from below. Moments later, a large slimy tentacle burst through the surface of the sea and then dove back below, turning to violently smash into the hull from below. The skiff lifted from the surface and abruptly shifted, sending Samara, Takashi, and Virgil sprawling into the ocean. Nara, latched in place on the skiff by Mech, screamed in terror. "Virgil!"

Samara barely heard the shriek as she rapidly sunk below the surface. She clawed at the gel, but it gave her no traction. The momentum of her descent slowed, and Samara came to a stop about eight feet below the surface. Panicking, she attempted to swim but couldn't provide the force to propel her body upwards against the weird texture and shifting density of the organism she was now immersed in. Still holding her breath, she struggled in place. Her lungs ached as she desperately tried to hang on to the last bit of air she had in her. That was short-lived as a streamlined hulk of grey with three bony fins placed equidistant around its body grazed against her body on its way by. The force knocked the air from her, and her lungs, starved for more, instinctively took a deep breath and inhaled a large gulp of the Zumerian organism.

The gel-filled her throat and lungs with a rush of warmth as her brain exploded with fear and dread. She prayed that her death would be swift and not the agonizing torturous pain of suffocation. By the time this thought ended, she unexpectedly realized that she was still capable of conscious thought. Was this what death was like? A gentle easing into the next life? A warm embrace devoid of terror and pain? She could still feel and think. Certainly not what she expected. Maybe this was the light that near-death survivors spoke of, and at any moment she would leave her body and bid it farewell for the trappings of eternity.

She felt a violent tug at her midsection. Not exactly the sensation she expected. A moment later, she was spun around to find Virgil gesturing wildly at her within the gel. He was mouthing something as he pointed at her waist. It was then that it finally sunk in that she wasn't dying. She took another breath as more of the warm gel-filled her chest. There was none of the pain or discomfort that she *should* have been feeling. Her body, though unaccustomed to breathing something like the gel, took to it like it was a natural act.

Virgil tugged at her lifeline and then pointed upwards, and she instantly understood what he wanted. Grabbing hold of the cable, she jerked it toward her until it went taut, then pulled herself toward the surface with Virgil doing the same by her side. They went up on their backs, nearly horizontally as the resistance of the gel fought them.

On the surface, the skiff remained afloat with Mech and Nara as its only passengers. Cables stretched out in three directions: two by the aft and one by the stern. Nara desperately tried to struggle free of Mech, but the robot held her too firmly and adeptly. "Let go of me!" she demanded. "I need to help them!"

Mech responded flatly, "Unable to process request."

A voice cried out. "Help me!" It was Takashi. He was half-submerged a reasonable distance away from the vessel. He pulled at his cable and wrenched himself free of the gel's grasp. Lying face down on the surface, it took all his control to not sink in again. He tried to remain completely still as he yelled to the others in the skiff. "Meg, Pull me in!"

The robot turned to Takashi's voice, with Nara still squirming to get loose. "Unable to process request," it informed the Tech Officer.

"Meg, help me!" ordered Takashi desperately.

"Unable to process request," repeated Mech, fully abiding by the order it was previously given directly by Takashi himself to protect Nara until they reached land with no room for exception.

Nara was aghast at the uselessness of this robot. From her point of view, it was disobeying a direct order. "Help him!" She insisted as she beat the droid. It simply compensated for the blows and remained fastened tight to her and the hull. Nara didn't understand that Mech was given no room for deviation in its last directive from Takashi, even to deal with their current situation.

A giant tentacle broke through the surface behind Takashi and loomed directly above him. The appendage had rows of hooked barbs surrounding mouth-like orifices covering most of its surface area. The tip fanned open, revealing a membranous web that undulated rapidly. Takashi felt the presence behind him and turned to see just as the tentacle whipped at him and wrapped around his torso, tightening like a constrictor. Takashi screamed in torturous pain as the trunk of the tentacle slid below and tugged at him to join the murky depths. "Meg!" he screamed in desperation.

Samara and Virgil surfaced on the other side of the skiff. As they struggled to get aboard, they heard screaming from beyond.

"Meg, help me!" the young officer shrieked, grabbing at his lifeline to stay afloat.

"Unable to process request," came the unemotional reply.

Nara was in full panic mode, but every time she managed

to wiggle loose a little, Mech would adjust its grip and pull her back in. "No!" she yelled at the robot. "You have to let me save him!" Mech just stared back at her blankly. Her words meant nothing to it. They didn't fit into the parameters of its command protocols as neatly as Takashi's from the beginning of their trip had.

Flopping over the side and onto the deck, Samara and Virgil immediately started vomiting up the organic sea. Between fits of heaving, Samara spied the action in the distance. As soon as she regained control of her body, she leaped for the taut cable that was tied onto Takashi and started pulling. "Takashi!" she called out to him. "Hang on!" Seconds later, Virgil joined in on the tug of war.

As the Tentacle solidified its grasp, Takashi's subsequent plea was choked with the sound of gurgling blood. His voice drowned in his wet throat. An awful snapping sound filled the air, and the cable suddenly went slack sending Samara and Virgil tumbling backward. They hit the far end, barely avoiding falling overboard again. Samara regained her footing with just enough time to see her friend's broken body dragged below and a pool of scarlet spread across the surface of the Sea. She averted her eyes as she was consumed by grief and nausea at the sight of what was left.

Pulling the lifeline into the skiff, Virgil studied the still intact loop. Takashi had been cut in two. Dropping the cable to the floor, he turned to Nara, who shielded her face with her hands. Mech's embrace provided no comfort whatsoever.

Virgil crossed to Samara. "We better keep moving," he said gently. "It'll be dark soon." She nodded, holding back the tears. She had liked Takashi very much and had looked forward to getting to know him when this was all over. Now that would never come to be.

Moments later, the engine roared, and the vessel continued toward the shore.

$\triangle\triangle\triangle$

Panya slipped in through the sliding doors of the tiny infirmary. Cradling a small clear plastic tub piled high with all sorts of tools and small devices, she crossed to the instrument panel and grabbed hold of the ultrasound device. Tugging hard, she yanked an attached coiled cord and disconnected it from its connection point to the panel. She then unceremoniously tossed the device into her box. With no time to spare, she was out the door.

As she exited the Magellan, she plopped down on the ground a few yards from Aden, who seemed to be conversing with the altricion again. The exterior lights were on, providing ample illumination to work by. Dumping out the contents of the plastic tub before her, Panya picked through the items and got to work disassembling a spare comm unit. The action caught Aden's attention, and he quietly studied Panya as she worked with skill and dexterity. She soon noticed that she was being watched but continued to stay focused on her task. "Don't you worry, captain," she said as she grabbed hold of the coiled cord of the ultrasound device and stripped the wires. "I'm going to show you why I was top of my class at the academy."

$\triangle\triangle\triangle$

Those that remained of the ground team appeared in a contemplative mood as the skiff exited the Zumerian Sea and drove up on the dry land. Virgil brought it to a slow halt just a few meters from the shoreline.

It was Mech who broke the silence as it retracted its hooks and finally loosened its grip on Nara with a mechanical hum.

Before the robot was finished, she managed to struggle loose and threw herself into her brother's arms. "Please inform Master Takashi that I am now able to process his request," spoke the machine without a hint of irony.

Somberly, Samara addressed Mech. "Takashi's not here."

"Shall I locate him for you?"

Erupting with frustration, she lunged toward the mechanoid with her hands balled up in fists. "He's dead, you fucking stupid piece-of-shit machine!" she spat out. "So you might as well erase him from your data banks! Get it?!"

Mech stared at her blankly with cold dead eyes. "Unable to process request."

"You could have saved him!" Her fist drew back.

Releasing Nara, Virgil jumped from his seat to break up the feud. "Samara. Relax," he insisted. "It doesn't understand. It only does what it's told."

Samara knew that, she didn't need to be reminded, but somehow hearing it from Virgil calmed her slightly.

"Shall I re-initialize my decision matrix?" asked Mech, utterly oblivious to the emotional turmoil it was causing.

Samara's hands unclenched and her arm dropped from its cocked position as she studied the robot for any signs of humanity or remorse. None were forthcoming. This was an exercise in futility, and Samara was done with trying to change things that were never meant to suit her in the first place. She had tried it for years with Aden, and look where that got her: trapped on an alien world with little hope for survival. "No... Meg," she said as she shook her head. "Resume Takashi's upgraded program." Samara intended to keep his memory alive.

CHAPTER SEVENTEEN

The altricion watched Panya curiously as she put the final touches on her cobbled-together apparatus. The main body of the device was made up of various parts of a comm and other scrounged gear. Connected to it was the coiled cord that led to the ultrasound wand. Altogether it looked like a makeshift Geiger counter built by an imaginative twelve-year-old.

As she stood up, she attached a long length of extra wire to the handle of the ultrasound wand and slowly approached Aden.

Aden watched her like a newborn child discovering the world for the first time as she pressed the ultrasound wand against his throat. He made no attempt to stop her. As a matter of fact, he seemed anxious to see where this venture was going, and to that end, he stayed utterly motionless so as not to dissuade her from finishing her task. Panya had no idea what was in control of Aden's body — him or the giant creature — but she knew they were now linked. If that were true, it might be possible to communicate with both of them and with the creature through Aden, similar to how the altricion seemed to.

Looping the wire around the back of his neck, Panya secured it to the other side of the device. It hung from him like a collar. Holding the rest of the gizmo in her hand, she stepped back from the captain, who was still connected via the coiled cord.

Taking a deep breath, she flipped a switch on the front panel, and the contraption hummed to life. A moment later, a burst of unwelcome static erupted from the speakers followed by an awful ear-piercing whine. She promptly adjusted the dials and leveled the sound out. Aden's body looked on, but the slug itself hadn't stirred.

Satisfied that she had dotted all the i's and crossed the t's, she looked Aden in the eyes, ready to go ahead with her experiment. "Captain," she said calmly. "Can you say your name?"

Aden paused as the wheels turned slowly in his muddled brain.

A long minute passed then suddenly, the comm squawked with life. "Aden," came a barely audible sound from the device's tiny speakers.

As Panya adjusted the volume, the altricion pawed at her leg. She leaned down to pick it up as Aden continued, "Samara..." he said in a modulated voice. "I need Samara."

The feral slug began to stir.

"We don't know where she is," replied Panya. Better to lay her cards out on the table. Besides, she was too exhausted to lie as the adrenaline coursing through her body started to wear off and the lack of sleep began to catch up. She yawned loudly as her eyelids started to flutter.

"Must find her," Aden continued.

Panya slowly lowered herself to the ground as another yawn escaped her lips. She was fading fast. "And what if she doesn't return?" she asked sluggishly.

The creature's tail tightened its grip on the Magellan as Panya drifted off, and the tiny altricion placed its paw on her chest. She dreamt of expansive forests full of massive growths that weren't *quite* trees and creatures that weren't *quite* animals that lived beneath them. She saw the comings and goings of Prime's two suns and one moon on the horizon, and the turning of its seasons. She saw the wonderous conglomeration of life on this planet, how it touched and interacted with the giant world itself. She saw the deep-down curiosity of Prime and everything on it, each part stretching out to learn, evolve, and grow.

Within the bowels of the ship, Wade lay on his bed, eyes closed. The sudden movement of the hull jarred him awake. Collecting himself, he got up and went to investigate. As he exited the ship, he spied Panya sitting cross-legged on the ground about five feet from Aden's re-animated corpse. Her head flopped over to the side. His first thought was that she was dead, but as he approached, he could hear her gently snoring. Inexplicably, Panya was sound asleep. What a tableau this was, thought Wade: This young girl blissfully napping mere feet from a monstrosity the likes that few humans will ever see. How the human mind can adapt so quickly from abject horror to complacency was a mystery. As he crossed behind her, he noticed the device that traced up from her hand to Aden's throat. His hand on her shoulder suddenly snapped her back to wakefulness. The Altricion retracted its tiny paw.

"What are you doing?!" he scolded her.

Still altered from her dream state, it took her a confused moment to respond, "I fell asleep."

He thrust out a finger toward the device in her hand. "You *what?* What is that thing?!"

Now back to her senses, Panya popped up from the ground and moved toward Aden. She didn't even pretend to hide the fact that she was ignoring his question. As far as Panya was concerned, she was in charge, even if her rank didn't imply it. The one-eyed man in the land of the blind is king, and she felt more than sure of her newly crowned royalty. She would now dictate policy, and Wade was on a need-to-know basis. She magnanimously decided to dole out a kernel to him. "He's obsessed with finding Samara," she stated in a matter-of-fact tone. "I don't think he intends to hurt us, but it might be out of his control. I'm not sure how much is him and how much is the creature in there."

Wade was unaccustomed to this overly confident side of Panya, and he didn't like it one bit. It reeked of insubordination, something he'd dealt with in spades from this crew. "Have you lost your mind?!" he barked at her. "How could you possibly know--"

Wade was cut off mid-sentence as the comm in Panya's hand erupted with noise, and Aden once again spoke. "Wade," said the eerily modulated voice.

Wade stopped dead in his tracks.

"Wade... I need Samara."

The XO panicked. This was way too much to process. "I want you to come inside with me *now*," he demanded as he grabbed Panya's wrist

"Let go of me!" she screamed as she pulled in her arm, trying to break free of his grasp, but Wade held her fast. "That's an order Panya."

"I'm not taking orders from you anymore!"

"What you're doing is wrong!" Wade pried the comm from Panya's grasp and tossed it by Aden's feet. "Leave him alone. He's fucking dead!" As he was dragging her back toward the Magellan, she shook free of him.

"Just don't touch me," she seethed bitterly. Scooping up the altricion, she stormed off to the ship.

"Just get some rest," Wade said. "We'll discuss this in the morning." He threw a cursory glance at his former captain and then made his way inside.

Wade walked swiftly to his quarters and, upon entering, went straight for a drawer by his bed. Sliding it open, he removed a well-worn pistol by the barrel. Seated on the corner of the bed, he inspected the weapon to ensure its proper condition and operation. The act was second nature to him. He knew this particular firearm as if it were an extension of his own body.

It had been with him through wars and bore almost as many scars as he did. Instead of replacing parts with brand-new ones, he took the time to fix and repair the existing ones when they became worn out. Outwardly, he did this because, to him, it was a sign of discipline, but his more deep-rooted reasons had to do with an innate opinion that just because something is damaged doesn't mean you toss it for the next thing. His gun had character. It had real experience and never let him down.

His index finger slipped easily behind the trigger guard. There was business to take care of.

$$\triangle\triangle\triangle$$

Parked by a narrow mountain range, the skiff's engine still hummed with life. Samara, seated with Mech and Nara, awaited Virgil's return, and passed the time by concentrating on keeping warm in the brisk night air.

Footsteps approached the vehicle.

"This is a good place," said Virgil as he emerged from the darkness. "It's too dangerous to travel at night." He shut the engines down.

Using supplies found on the vehicle, a makeshift tent had been erected between the truck and the side of the small mountain. A healthy fire crackled with life, which Samara maintained with unmistakable fervor. Mech was standing guard, rotating on her torso to slowly scan the surrounding environment. Her arms were raised in front of her, and her hands, now reconfigured to expose their internal sensors, were out in front. Nara sat across from Samara at the fire while Virgil huddled in the skiff, assessing the data deck's storage drive for damage or errors. Satisfied with the fire, Samara leaned back and wrapped herself up in her arms. She studied Nara and then turned to watch Virgil hovering over his valued possession.

"He's the only family I've got," informed Nara as she watched Samara studying her brother.

"Huh?"

"When I signed up for this assignment, he refused to let me go without him."

"I didn't know you were allowed to bring family," remarked Samara. She had no basis for this assumption but wanted to carry on the conversation to keep her mind free from having to focus on the unpleasant situation they were currently in.

"You're not," answered Nara, to Samara's surprise. "Virgil's one of best exobiologists in the field. They were glad to have him."

Samara nodded.

"I don't think I would have made it if he hadn't come." Nara let the comment hang in the chilled air before changing the subject. "Where's your family?"

Samara laughed to herself as if Nara had made an obvious joke. "You're looking at it."

"You have friends?" inquired Nara, not seeing the amusement in her query.

"I guess."

"Someone you love?" pressed the young girl.

Samara smiled wryly at the bluntness of the question. "Let's say... someone I... yeah," she responded vaguely.

"So, you feel you're obliged to be with this guy?" asked Nara, generally interested.

"I didn't say that!" Unwittingly, Nara had pressed one of Samara's hidden buttons.

"I'm not trying to upset you," said Nara to calm her. "It's refreshing to have a conversation with another woman that isn't about science." The last thing she wanted to do was to make Samara clam up, so she continued cautiously and chose her words with a little more care. "You just seem... kind of unhappy, that's all."

"Well, you probably would be, too, if you lived most of your life aboard the same damn spaceship," spat Samara bitterly.

"Why don't you leave?" asked Nara. "Get away for a while?" It seemed a reasonable question.

"It's more complicated than that," rebutted Samara.

"It's only as complicated as you make it," replied Nara with an air of self-righteousness that made Samara's hackles stand on end.

The conversation was over as far as Samara was concerned, "Do me a favor and stick to analyzing the creatures."

"I didn't--"

Suddenly Mech stopped rotating at the waist, and its arms repositioned. "Proximity alert."

Samara and Nara froze in place as Virgil looked up from the data deck.

"Meg, what is it?" asked Samara cautiously.

"Bipedal organism, approximately six meters long, current course intersects with our position," stated Mech unemotionally. "At its current velocity, it will arrive in approximately two minutes."

Samara got to her feet. "Shit!"

With the data deck tucked firmly under his arm, Virgil slowly exited the skiff. "Don't panic. It's probably a rawboned zephyr." He quickly crossed to Samara and his sister. "They use echolocation to navigate and hunt. If we stay still and don't pose a threat, it'll likely mind its own business."

"We should load up the truck," suggested Samara as the

thumping of hooves approached.

"There's no time," warned Virgil.

"Aren't these the things that wiped out most of your camp?!"

"Just do what I say," instructed Virgil, trying to keep his voice low. As he moved in closer to Nara, Samara drew her weapon and stood ready. "I'm warning you Samara. Don't move." He was getting exasperated with her. He knew these creatures well, and the way she was behaving was going to get all of them seriously injured or killed.

Nara slowly wrapped her good arm around Virgil's waist. She also knew these creatures all too well, having lived firsthand through one of their vicious attacks on the camp. They had left her wounded, and her friends and colleagues butchered.

Suddenly the trees parted, and a lissome mammal with a pendulous swag-bellied frame entered the clearing. The rawboned zephyr slowed its pace and came to a complete halt. Using its branched raspy horn, it dug at the ground and huffed a few times. Steam rose from a multitude of tiny nostrils that peppered its angular head and provided vision for this sightless beast. Along its back there were solid plates, armoring it like something made for war. Its name was apt — at the tip of its tails, two raw bony spikes protruded. Samara couldn't tell which was more frightening – its horns or those tails.

Lifting its long neck, the zephyr produced a rhythmic pinging sound that broke the stillness. Patiently, the barbed creature collected its data. Each cycle of pings frayed Samara's nerves as she struggled to stay still. Even in the cold night air, sweat beaded on her brow.

As her hand pressed up against the data deck under Virgil's arm, Nara squeezed his waist tighter. Like Samara, her palms were moist with sweat.

The zephyr locked onto something... the movement of

collapsing wood in the center of the dancing flames of the fire. Hungry for sustenance, the creature readied its attack.

Virgil knew this would end badly. Once the creature realized its mistake and received a nasty burn from the flames, it would go ballistic. They were standing too close and certainly would receive some of the fallout. He made a decision. Ever so quietly, he spoke in a whispered hush to his sister. He tried to move his mouth as little as possible. "Nara, Listen." With limited movement, he very slowly slid the data deck into her good arm. "Make sure this makes it back to Earth in one piece."

Before she could even realize what he was up to, Virgil bolted away from the camp and screamed at the beast while waving his arms wildly in the air. "Look at me, you bastard!" he yelled at the top of his lungs. "Look at me!"

"Virgil! *No!*" screamed Nara.

As he sprinted away from them, the zephyr howled ferociously, then charged, galloping after its prey. Virgil raced toward a wall of rock as the zephyr closed the distance. Before he could dodge the blow, the creature's bony head smacked into Virgil's side, sending him flying against the jagged rocks. Severely battered, he fell to the ground unconscious. The zephyr made a wide turn to reposition for the kill and once again charged. It gathered momentum as it sped headfirst toward its easy prey.

A bright blast smacked the charging beast in the hindquarters. The wound was small but enough to slow it down. Whipping its head around, it turned its attention to the new menace: Samara. Changing its course, it now galloped toward her.

The gun shook in her hand as the creature charged toward her. It would be only a matter of seconds before she was trampled to death or skewered on its barbed antlers. Her finger flexed on the trigger and rapidly fired two shots. It took three more to take the beast down. It crashed into the dirt, and it made a horrible sound. Keeping the gun trained on the creature, Samara motioned to Nara. She had no clue whether this thing was actually dead or not, and she wasn't about to do anything stupid like assume the best and learn the hard way. "Go help your brother," she instructed the younger girl.

With the data deck under her arm, Nara ran along the stone wall as fast as she could to her fallen sibling. "Virgil?!" she cried as she closed the distance.

The sound of his sister's voice penetrated the darkness, and his eyes began to flutter open. His eyes attempted to focus on the person rushing toward him, but the world was blurred and muddled, a lingering side effect of the blow to his head.

"Virgil!" she continued to yell in her distorted voice. Then it abruptly stopped.

With only a few yards to go, Nara was suddenly gone... vanished into thin air.

The terrifying confusion that came next caused a rush of adrenaline to course through Virgil's system, giving him a sudden boost of clarity. "Nara?" Said Virgil as he tried to rise from the ground. Where did she go?

Inhuman movement from the stone wall to his right attracted his attention. Entrenched in the rocks, a large mimesis retracted its claws from its gaping maw and began to chew its prey. Blood and chunks of meat dribbled from its mouth as bones crunched in its teeth. There was no sound from Nara — no screams of shock or howls of pain. Just the crunching and wet ripping that came from the monster's mouth. She was gone as soon as it had impaled her with its giant spear-like front appendages. The meal was its reward.

Virgil's eyes went wide with shock. "Oh, God! No!" he screamed in stunned agony at the image before him. He froze.

Spurred by the screaming, Samara ditched the dead zephyr and raced toward Virgil. "Meg, follow me!" she instructed the mech as she raced at top speed. As they arrived by Virgil's side, they saw the full extent of the horror of the moment. What was left of Nara was now on the ground, on Virgil, and everywhere.

On autopilot, Samara lifted her weapon and let loose a barrage of fire at the creature's mid-section tearing it apart. As it died, the mimesis regurgitated a large globular form from its mouth. Covered in a green sticky slime, Nara's torso still twitched. The scene seemed ripped from a nightmare. Next to her laid the data deck, unharmed by the molecular acid of the mimesis' fluids.

Virgil gasped for air as he collapsed in a piteous heap. Tears streaked from his eyes. Nara was dead. She was gone forever. He was unable to save her. He felt numb and empty.

There was suddenly more movement within the stone wall directly beyond him. Not a moment later, a full-grown adult mimesis appeared and began to extricate itself from the rock face. Its large sword-like appendages searched for prey. In comparison to the first, it was even more massive.

Samara grabbed Virgil by the arm and tried to hoist him from the ground, but he was a lump of dead weight that had given up its will to live over the soul-crushing loss of his beloved sister.

"Get up!" she barked at him.

He still wouldn't budge, so she dug her nails deep into his flesh. "Snap out of it, Virgil!" she demanded. Samara wasn't going down like this, but she also wasn't going to let Virgil throw his life away, either. They had come too far together. "She's dead, and if we don't move now, we're dead too!"

Virgil's survival mode suddenly kicked in, and the beast continued to free itself from the rocks. Samara, Virgil, and Mech rushed toward the skiff.

Suddenly, Virgil dug his heels in and came to an abrupt

stop. "The deck!"

"Screw it!" she screamed incredulously.

Virgil was beyond listening to her. Breaking free, he raced back to the rocks just as the mimesis cleared them. Ripping off his overshirt as he ran, he used it to protect his hands as he scooped up the acid-drenched data deck.

The mimesis immediately locked in on him and whipped one of its sharp hunting appendages directly toward him. Barely avoiding the dagger-like spike, Virgil changed course back to the skiff and sped up to a full sprint with the gargantuan beast in tow.

Leaving the tent and supplies behind, Samara revved up the vehicle as Mech situated itself in the back. She turned to see Virgil running toward them with the silver case grasped in his hands and the sizeable crab-like mimesis lumbering behind in pursuit. It was faster than she expected.

She gunned the skiff and sped toward him. The mimesis swatted at Virgil with its spiked arms, but he was able to bob and weave and stay free of harm. Getting a bead on the oncoming skiff, Virgil prepared himself to jump. He'd get one chance at this. If he missed, he'd be dead for sure.

Samara cut the wheel as the vehicle's tires scraped against the ground and kicked up a plume of dust and dirt that billowed toward the creature's face. The distraction gave Virgil a few more precious moments. With the last vestiges of his adrenaline-fueled strength, he catapulted himself into the back of the truck.

"Go...Go...Go!!!" he implored her.

Not remotely needing the instruction, Samara once again floored it and sped at top speed into the forest.

The mimesis, locked on a tasty meal, pursued with extreme vigor and determination.

CHAPTER EIGHTEEN

Eyes closed but ready for action, Wade sat on his bed with his back to the wall. He held the gun in his lap with his finger on the trigger.

"NTSS Magellan," crackled the ship's comm. "This is the URS Paladin. Do you copy?"

Wade's eyes snapped open as he reached for the comm, "Go for Magellan."

"We have entered Prime's orbit and will be sending down the shuttle within the hour," came the friendly reply.

"Perfect."

"The corporation has been contacted, and they'll handle the salvage," added the Paladin's Comms Officer. "I sure hope your bosses have good insurance. Paladin out."

With the gun in hand, Wade rose from the bed and exited his room. He had only one thought in his head now: it was time.

ΔΔΔ

As the primary sun rose behind them, Samara raced the skiff through the dense forest. Virgil huddled in the back with Mech as the mimesis continued to follow at speed.

"Meg, protect this at all costs," commanded Virgil as he placed the data deck into Mech's arms. "Do not let go of it until instructed."

The robot obediently complied. "Affirmative, Sir."

$$\triangle\triangle\triangle$$

Wade walked cautiously toward Aden, who continued to kneel in the dirt in the same position as the night before. With Panya's device still attached to his throat, he looked up as Wade approached.

"Wade... where is Samara?" asked Aden in an off-putting modulated voice.

Stopping a few paces away, Wade raised the gun and trained it on his former captain's head. "I'm sorry, Aden," he began. "It's better for all of us this way." He didn't expect this to be as difficult as he imagined when he planned it back in his cabin. Aden was dead. This *thing* before him was an abomination. An echo of a good man, at best. There was no reason for hesitation. This was the right decision.

He swallowed hard as he worked up the courage to squeeze the trigger and finally put an end to all this.

$$\triangle\triangle\triangle$$

Determined to make it back to the Magellan, Samara stayed focused on the road ahead. "We've got to be close," she said more as a reassurance to herself than to the others. She was correct. Not a moment later, the trees began to thin out and a clearing could be spotted beyond. As the mimesis roared from the rear, she rode the throttle harder even though the pedal was already on the floor.

As they burst from the forest, they immediately saw the

Magellan. It lay where they left it, but most of the hull was obscured by a massive Slug-like creature holding firm to its rear section. The hull was breached, with tears in it from the stress of the giant animal's brutal force. It was dented, dinged, battered, and banged up, sitting on its crushed landing gear like an animal with all its legs broken.

Samara's face contorted at the bizarre sight. "What the--"

Before she could finish the thought, The mimesis' spear-like front arm dug into the back wheel of the skiff, barely missing Virgil's head. Samara lurched forward as the front wheels turned abruptly, then flipped the vehicle when the mimesis retracted its limb. The passengers were thrown from the truck and landed hard on the ground.

Fortunately for them, the mimesis was occupied with the destruction of the skiff. The loud noise and commotion nearby drew Wade's attention, but with his view blocked by the slug and still single-minded in his thoughts, he did not bother to investigate its cause.

Suddenly, Panya appeared at the main hatch with the altricion on her shoulder. "What was that...." Her eyes went wide as she saw Wade with the gun pointed directly at Aden's forehead. "Wade!" she screamed. "What the hell are you doing?!" She ran toward him, hoping to stop him before he had a chance to fire.

"Stay back!" he ordered as he steadied the gun.

As the mimesis continued to eviscerate the skiff beyond his view, Virgil helped Samara to her feet, and they stumbled on toward the disabled ship with Mech in tow. They were in rough shape and in absolutely no condition to defend themselves if the creature attacked again.

"We can still get to the ship," said Virgil frantically. Their only hope at this point was to get to the relative safety and shelter of the ship, which from their vantage point, didn't look all that safe after all.

"What is that thing?!" demanded Samara, referring to the giant worm-like body holding onto their only hope of salvation.

"It's a feral slug," answered Virgil. "They're not supposed to be local to this area."

"Is it going to attack us?" asked Samara, even though she was currently racing straight toward the belly of the beast.

"I don't know," was Virgil's best guess. What he saw before him seemed to be very odd behavior for a feral slug. Then again, based on everything he'd witnessed in the last few days, anything was possible.

As they came around to the opposite side of the slug while giving it a wide berth, they immediately beheld an even weirder sight. The impending execution of Aden Harker by his XO.

Time stood still for Samara as her brain, already bombarded by too much new information, suddenly had to process something beyond her wildest expectations. Aden's odd appearance or the weird appendage attached to his skull didn't even register with her. "No!!!" was all she could muster.

Panya was too shocked by the sudden reappearance of Samara to react as the drama unfolded before her.

Sprinting like a horse out of the gate, Samara closed the impossible distance in no time. As she got closer Wade and the gun came into razor-sharp focus.

Just as Wade turned to see her coming, she tackled him to the ground. The gun bounced on the soil, and Samara, flushed with adrenaline, snatched it up and aimed it at Wade.

"Samara, wait!" pleaded Wade as he held his hands out toward her. "*He's not Aden anymore!*"

Turning her head to study Aden, reality seeped in. Wade was telling the truth. There was something *wrong* here. This wasn't her mentor, her friend, her lover. It looked like him, but something... something was not quite right. His expression had none of the life and vigor she had known him for. His deep brown eyes had lost their glint, their fire. As if in a trance, Samara let the gun slip from her hand. Slowly, she crossed to Aden and, with only a few feet left, collapsed to her knees directly in front of him. "Aden?" she muttered, staring him in the face, searching his eyes.

There was a long moment then he spoke, "You came back to me." He gazed at her with sadness in those eyes as he stretched his arms out to her. Samara trembled with anguish as her body betrayed her.

"I needed to tell you...." he began to say when suddenly she embraced him tightly, drawing him close. "Let me go," he said with the same modulated, emotionless voice.

"I'm not ready..." she cried. "I'm scared...." A single tear traced down her cheek. "I never told you how much I love you... You saved my life...."

Aden's expression remained stone cold. "You saved me, too," he said. "Now, let me go."

His hands found Samara's face and grasped her firmly. She instantly froze in terror as he drew her even closer. Did he mean to harm her? Her body suddenly began to spasm as she took in the rest of the details of Aden's current disposition. Things that had only been seen and registered by her subconscious came to her waking awareness and, with them, brought the horror of the moment.

Simultaneously, the feral slug stirred, and its tail began to tighten around the Magellan's hull. The metal ship strained to hold its form against the massive amount of pressure being laid upon it. The screech of metal strained against its limit filled the immediate area, and Panya quickly raced away from the ship in fear of its imminent destruction. "Samara!" she cried out in the hope that she could somehow break the spell and make it stop.

Without warning, the skiff suddenly hurled past them. It was followed by the unwelcome arrival of the mimesis.

Virgil backed up to Panya as the creature advanced. As he turned to her, he noticed the altricion perched on her shoulder. The appearance of the tiny creature was so unexpected he almost couldn't believe his luck. Grabbing hold of the tiny organism, Virgil snatched it from her, but before he could get away, she seized his arm tightly. "What are you doing?!" she demanded. Was this guy out of his mind? This was her friend that he had just taken.

"Let go of me!" yelled Virgil, having no time to explain his actions.

"You're going to hurt him!"

Incensed by this woman, Virgil got in her face, "It's our only chance! Let go of me!"

Wrenching free of her hold, he raced toward the attacking mimesis with the altricion cupped in his hands. Panya was so flustered she didn't know what to do. By the time she even considered chasing after him, he was already in striking distance of the menace that was trying to kill them all.

Unphased by the mimesis attack, Samara continued to plead with Aden, "I need you!" she cried, unwilling to accept his words.

"Then you'll die..." was his matter-of-fact reply.

The feral slug's tail squeezed tighter around the Magellan. The hull was close to outright collapse as thick metal began to fold inward.

Wade watched as the events transpired before him. Suddenly a realization washed over him. With no time to waste, he scrambled over to Samara. "He wants you to live your life," he told her emphatically, but she either wasn't listening or chose to ignore him. "Samara. Listen to me," he begged her.

Virgil was completely unaware of the drama closer to the feral slug; his main and only concern was the mimesis. It meant to devour them all, and it was now up to him to make sure that didn't happen, even if it meant putting himself in harm's way. Dropping to his knees before the enormous attacking beast, he stretched his arms into the air lifting the altricion high above his head.

Panya was almost delirious with horror. "No!!!" He was going to sacrifice her only friend in this hellhole of a place to the attacking monster. She looked around her for any means to stop him, but she was utterly helpless to do so.

The giant creature loomed above Virgil and pounced.

Just before its mouth could reach its prey, the mimesis violently jerked backward as if a heavy plasma bolt had hit it. A horrific howl erupted from its gaping maw as it suddenly began to thrash around in agony.

Panya watched, unsure of what was happening. From her point of view, she couldn't hear the piercing psychic howl of the altricion directed solely at the mimesis. She could only witness its impact as the beast continued to writhe in pain.

Impulsively, the mimesis made a last-ditch effort to lunge at the altricion but was only met with further resistance as a gut-wrenching expulsion of psychic noise erupted in its brain. Its eyes bled greenish goo. It screamed.

The thrashing and screaming suddenly gave way to a choked rasp, and then it was over. The mimesis fell to the ground as acid and bile seeped from its mouth and body, searing the soil. It was dead.

The danger was far from over.

Still in Aden's grasp, Samara's body continued to tremble as she was lifted to a standing position. Panya's device slipped off his throat and crashed to the ground, and a silent scream choked at the back of Samara's throat.

As Virgil raced over to the others, he handed Panya back the altricion. The tiny creature was unharmed. He crossed next to Wade to see if there was anything he could do but realized quickly that it was all up to Samara.

Wade pleaded with her one last time, "Please, Samara," he said gently. *"Let him go."*

Tears flowed freely as Samara looked deep into her lover's eyes. It was devastating to utter the following words, but Wade was right; this was the only way to set them both free.

"You'll always be a part of me."

Suddenly, everything stopped.

A loud noise behind them prompted them to turn. The feral slug's tail unexpectedly released the rear of the Magellan. Its appendages relaxed and swung back around, retracting closer to its body. The tips of its tentacle-like "arms" had started to pulsate. The creature's body rapidly heaved and contorted as bulges appeared under its skin and traveled toward them below the surface. The globes were multicolored, some light and others dark, as they moved beneath its translucent skin.

Then something amazing happened.

A large bead of clear resin bubbled out from between the two pulsating tips and was deposited on the ground. As the appendages moved away from the glob, more of the clear liquid poured out and added to the shape.

Virgil, Wade, and Panya watched in amazement as a definitive form began to take shape. The more liquid resin the creature deposited, the more the vision was realized.

As the work continued, the feral slug began to emit a low hum, almost like the vibration of an engine turbine. It resonated in their very bones like a distant song. Tears streaked down Samara's face, and her expression suddenly shifted from fear to wonder. Panya, in amazement, felt the tiny altricion hum back. She was caught between them and felt a slow pulsing in the back of her mind, around and beneath everything. She finally understood – the beast, the planet, the altricion, Aden – all of it was connected. The psychic fields of Vega Prime weren't for sharing data, thoughts, or ideas – they were how its denizens shared memories and feelings. Now these humans were in them, part of them, and connected too.

Transfixed by the movements of the slug's appendages, no one moved a muscle as it composed its sculpture. The elegant curves of resin and the air trapped inside formed images that traced the growth of a young crystalline girl as she grew to maturity. Each meter of the ever-growing piece of art aged her form and features. By the halfway point, the carefree girl was recognizable as Samara. Further down, the happy smiles faded to bitter tears. But then a male figure appeared in the molten conglomeration and embraced the girl. Her sad look was soon replaced by one of contentment and even pleasure as the slug continued to shape the massive diorama.

A moan escaped Samara's lips as she and Aden were slowly returned to the ground by the creature's strange protuberance. When they reached it, the feral slug's construction finally ceased.

All eyes fell on Samara as Aden's hands loosened from her and dropped to his side.

A curious look appeared on her face: not sadness or pain. Understanding. She, too, understood what Panya had realized.

Slowly, she turned to her friends.

It was Panya who broke the eerie silence. "Samara?"

Samara cocked her head introspectively, then looked back to Aden.

The group collectively let out a sigh. It seemed that the danger had come and gone, leaving them all with a weirdly drained sense of calm.

Virgil took the lull to cross to Mech and finish his business. "Meg, release the data deck," he instructed the robot.

Mech uncurled its arms and presented the case to him as commanded.

As Virgil retrieved it, something out of the corner of his eye on the ground behind Mech caught his attention. He trotted over to the area to investigate. To his amazement, Virgil discovered the skeletal remains of the Slug's last victim. Recognizing the tattered uniform, he got down on one knee to confirm his unwanted suspicion. "It can't be."

Tugging at the torn clothes, he revealed a name tag. "McMasters." He said the name out loud as a barrage of answers flooded his head. This realization was more than just a confirmation of his colleague's death; it had a much more profound and ultimately devastating meaning. The creature hadn't just absorbed McMasters — it had somehow assimilated his mind, his anger, and maybe even his memories. Now it seemed it had also done that with Aden. A wave of despondency overtook him as he tried to make sense of this new information.

Rising to her feet, Samara surveyed the newly created resin sculpture. Awkwardly, Panya and Wade approached in front of her, partially obscuring her view. Looking past them to the monument that presented a collage of her life, she marveled at its beauty. She pushed by and approached it, touching a segment that represented her as a teenager holding onto Aden tightly. Upon further inspection, it was revealed that his eyes were actually full of grief.

"Are you alright?" asked Panya, noticeably concerned.

"Yeah," said Samara as she smiled for the first time in a long time. "I think I am."

A grunting bellow from the slug drew everyone's attention. They watched in silence as Aden's body lifted from the ground and was reclaimed by the worm. As the body disappeared inside the sac, the slug shifted its weight and moved away from them. Its body undulating it left a wide swath of flattened foliage and slime in its wake.

With a peaceful smile on her face, Samara watched the creature until it had completely vanished from her sight into the depths of the alien forest.

The altricion pawed at Panya's neck, and as she turned to it, she noticed Virgil's melancholy manner. Going to him, she met his gaze. "You must be Virgil," she said, realizing that they had never been formally introduced.

Still looking down at the remains of McMasters, Virgil nodded and then spoke with a pained expression, "Everything I thought I knew, everything I believed in...."

He gestured to the crystal sculpture. "This isn't a message...*it's an excretion.*"

Virgil dropped to the ground and placed the data deck by the remains of McMasters. The information it held was useless: Just some naive observations and assumptions.

"I learned nothing," he said as he turned to her solemnly.

Panya was oblivious to the significance of the gesture.

As Virgil stood up, he watched as the altricion tangled itself in Panya's hair. As the tiny creature fumbled about, he reached out and unstuck it for her. Virgil's movements were knowing and gentle. Stroking the altricion under one of its arms, it suddenly cooed with pleasure.

It was a new sound, one that Panya had not heard from the altricion before. The noise was loving and pleasant, and it vaguely reminded her of the sound a newborn baby makes. Virgil knew precisely how to prompt this joy from the tiny creature. "I wouldn't say you learned nothing," she said to him warmly.

△△△

A loud sonic boom from above demanded everyone's attention. They looked up into the brightness of the suns as the silhouette of a large shuttlecraft descended toward them. It landed in the field behind the Magellan. The engines idled with a vibrating grumble as a ramp extended from the hull.

Samara turned to Wade, "I assume that's the cavalry."

"I'm not going with you," he said without hesitation.

"What?" This was the last thing she was expecting to hear. Her eyes traced down as she noticed the gun in his hand. What was he planning on doing? Suicide? Wade Fassell didn't just roll over and die or crawl under some rock. He was a fighter. Whether Samara liked to admit it or not, they were cut from the same cloth: *stubborn as all hell*. As much as she felt for his grief, this was not a fitting end for her adversary. He deserved to live. He had earned it. She looked him in the eyes. They were filled with sadness, but mostly they were filled with exhaustion: too many years of hardship and loss. Too much trauma. She knew that look. It was hers. "Wade," she said gently, "Everything's going to be alright now."

There was a pregnant pause.

"He gave you absolution?" asked Wade.

Samara now understood what Wade wanted. Like her, he needed to be free of the past. Like her, he needed to just let it go.

"Yes," she said emphatically, nodding her head.

He simply nodded, then holstered the weapon, turning to the trail left by the Slug. Placing a comforting hand on his shoulder, Samara gave him a brief squeeze. "I hope you find what you're looking for out there." There was a new light in his eyes.

Wade knew his next journey, his next life, began as he traveled down that path. This was *right*. It was time for something new.

Samara crossed to their mech and delivered her final order, "Stay with him, Meg. Make sure he finds his way home."

"Affirmative," replied the robot as it turned and obediently followed Wade into the forest. Soon they were gone from her sight. She hoped she would see them again someday soon.

Turning toward Panya and Virgil, she headed for the shuttle. As they arrived at the ramp, a rescue medic flanked by two armed soldiers appeared at the hatch and met them halfway.

The Medic surveyed the immediate area. "I was told there was only one of you," he shouted over the din of the engines. "Are there any others besides you three?"

Panya looked around, confused. "Where's Wade?" she asked Samara.

Samara turned to Panya and shook her head. Panya seemed to understand. "Three people," she said definitively to the Medic. "It's just the three of us."

The man nodded as one of the soldiers pointed to the tiny creature in Virgil's hand. "Sir, that thing can't come with us," he said respectfully. "Regulations."

Virgil looked to Panya, "It wouldn't survive if you took it with you."

Handing the altricion to her, Virgil guided them to the edge of the forest and found a small path.

Holding back her tears, Panya kissed the tiny creature and rubbed her cheek against its soft flesh. The feeling was comforting to her. It felt right.

She then lowered it to the ground and slowly released her hold.

"It's called an altricion," explained Virgil.

Panya watched it stumble off into the woods.

"We named them that because they're helpless when they're born. They need another organism to care for them until they're ready." He then smiled at her warmly. "It looks like you did a good job."

Panya smiled back.

"I'm having a baby," she said with conviction.

Filled with renewed confidence, Panya headed back toward the shuttle and, passing by Samara, disappeared inside.

As Virgil walked up the ramp, he turned to Samara. "What about your ship?" he asked.

Samara took one last look at the Magellan, her surrogate home for those many years, "I'll come back to it when I'm ready." She walked onto the rescue ship followed by Virgil as the hatch sealed shut behind them.

The Shuttle's engines revved up and a blast of flames propelled it skyward. As it ascended to the stars, it departed in the light of the new day.

EPILOGUE

Trailing behind the slug, Wade worked his way down the path it cut while deep in thought. He contemplated the events of the last few days. He pondered his choices, seeing them clearly for what they were: some good, some bad, all human. He thought about Panya, who had grown before his eyes in a day. He thought of Samara, his equal in every way that he could never accept. He thought of Takashi, lost to the literal confines of his own work. Most of all, he thought about Aden.

Aden Harker had been his student, then his peer, then his boss. More than that, he had been his friend. Wade intended to understand what became of Aden at the end and to see that there was closure for both of them. After all Wade had said and done on this voyage, he could do one thing to make it right — he could make sure his friend and shipmate was at peace. If that were his last act, it would be more worthy than any blaze of glory he had sought. Wade finally understood what he had gotten wrong for so long, that he had to prove himself *to himself* and not anyone else. He could reclaim some of what he'd lost and move on in that way. Or at least he hoped so.

△△△

The tiny yellowish creature waddled behind the Mech, trying to keep up, its stumpy little legs pounding the soil at an impossible speed for something so small. It was no use. It stopped in its tracks and chittered to itself, seemingly losing hope. At the sound, Mech stopped, turned, and looked down at the little creature behind it. "Do you require assistance?" the machine asked. As it waited for a reply, the tiny critter chittered again, then started climbing up the Mech's body.

In the distance behind him, Wade heard the mechanoid's servos moving in time with its steps. It wasn't fast, so he decided to wait for it and see what was happening. He had watched the shuttle take off earlier from his vantage point on the broad path and assumed everyone who had survived was on it. If the Mech had been left behind, it was more likely a choice made by Samara than some oversight. If it was following him, it had been expressly instructed to do so.

As the Mech came closer, it slowed its pace even further, following a path that would put it directly in front of him. Wade noticed the tiny yellowish addition to Mech's equipment as it neared. He froze. The creature had hurt him and tortured his mind in his worst moments to get him to stop his temporary insanity and protect Panya. It was dangerous. He knew that. He was at a loss for how to proceed.

The tiny creature jumped down from Mech, shuffled over to Wade, and raised its hands. Its body was animated, and it was chittering excitedly. It reminded Wade of a small child or a puppy in some profound and primal way, and his sense of threat seemed to dissolve. After a moment, he grew inquisitive, realizing that this tiny being was a part of the greater picture of the events of recent days. He picked it up. Then he froze stone still, like a statue, as its gills parted, and it began to *sing*. The song was in his head, something only he could hear. It was beautiful, and as the small creature wrapped the tiny fingers of one hand around one of Wade's scarred and gnarled digits, Wade finally saw.

His mind swam, but it was a gentle wandering through thought and memory that felt safe. He felt the presence of the tiny creature and knew this was its doing. Memories flooded by — some his and some the altricion's. He saw what it had seen, not just recently but since it was born. He saw the ebb and flow of life on Vega Prime. He saw his crew, and he saw Panya. He saw her depth and humanity in the face of the horrors they had encountered. He saw Aden, not alive, not dead, still connected to the giant slug providing it with sensory data, memories, and experiences. He saw the altricion commune with the slug through Aden, sharing its memories of the people inside the ship and its awareness of the helpless growing life inside Panya. He saw it all. As the images faded, he wept, and the small creature sang to him.

△△△

Back on the move, Wade could tell from the fresh slime on top of the soil that he was getting closer to the feral slug. The thing wasn't that far ahead now. He wondered what he would do when he caught up to it, how the creature would react. Mostly, he wondered what he'd say to Aden. As he rounded a bend, he halted in his tracks, face to face with the creature which had stopped moving and turned back at the sound of the man. He stood there stock still, waiting to see who moved first. The slug did.

Out of the pouch on its upper section, the insectoid arm carrying Aden Harker extended, drawing his slowly decaying body from within. It stopped directly in front of Wade and blinked silently. "Aden, can you hear me, buddy? Are you in there?" he said. There was nothing, just another slow blink, no comprehension. In his mind, he thought that the Aden in there was fading. He put his hand to his gun and made up his mind.

The altricion had other ideas. It sauntered between them, directly in the middle of the pair, and with its arms it gestured to Wade. Wade knelt, and as he did, Aden's corpse lowered to join him. The small yellow creature beckoned him closer, and when he leaned all the way in, it snatched his finger in one of its hands. In the other, it was holding Aden's. As the two beings connected through the Altricion, Wade knew exactly what needed to be said.

"It's time, Aden. It's time to let go." The slug quivered in response, and Aden once again blinked. Wade looked at the slug and, with his mind as much as his mouth, said, "This is wrong. He's gone. Please let him go." After a moment or two, the slug quivered again, then lifted Aden to his full height. It found a level spot, laid him on the soil, and released the appendage that had hooked into his cranium. Aden's body twitched once, and then finally, truly died. Wade was grateful, and as the altricion let go of his finger, he said "Thank you" to the tiny creature.

ΔΔΔ

Wade had buried Aden in a small clearing off the path in the forest at the edge of the marsh as the feral slug and tiny creature looked on. He did it with his bare hands and some sharp sticks he found in the woods, nothing more. Aden was finally laid to rest.

As he set back toward the path, the slug inched its bulk closer to him. It would be what it would be, he thought. He wondered if, in a moment, a thousand hooks would rip through his skull and link to his brain, hijacking his nervous system. He didn't care. What needed to be done was done. He had proven himself to himself.

When the slug got to him, it came extremely close, closer than it ever had before. As Wade waited and wondered what his fate would be, the appendage that had linked with Aden reappeared. The hooked and barbed end was now in front of him, pulsating in front of his face. It had Aden's blood on it still.

As Wade prepared himself, something odd happened before his eyes. The ring of hooks around the tip of the appendage that had suspended Aden retracted, revealing small, delicate tendrils waving around inside. These tendrils slowly drifted forth, wandering this way and that toward Wade's face. He stayed still as they finally reached him, touching and caressing his cheeks and brow. Suddenly, the tendrils connected to his skin and through the nerves in his skin to the rest of his nervous system. The two were now linked in the way it and Aden had been, but Wade had come to no harm. Through Wade and through the altricion, it had learned something about humanity, and this attempt at communicating showed that the slug-like creature had evolved. Wade settled in and opened his mind to the creature.

ΔΔΔ

Two weeks later, with its new Captain and mechanoid helmsman, the NTSS Magellan lifted off from the surface of Vega Prime and rocketed upwards into the heavens. It looked nothing like it had before. Where there were holes in the hull, there were now layers of ultra-strong resin. Where conduits were damaged, tube-like tentacles had been grown in their place. The parts of the ship that the feral slug had destroyed had, for the most part, been repaired using materials and methods unique to Prime mixed with Wade's experience and ingenuity. He didn't do it alone; his new acquaintances had helped.

Far away from Earth, Wade Fassell piloted the ship out of Vega Prime's atmosphere and toward a nearby cluster of stars teeming with habitable planets in their orbits. He was ready to begin a new adventure.

ΔΔΔ

Darkness obscured the dorsal section of the creature as it

emerged from the murky depths of the gelatinous Zumerian Sea. As the behemoth slowly rose, gel cascaded off its coarse flesh and rejoined the vast ocean below. Gradually, the shape lumbered toward the shore.

Composed of bizarre tree-like vegetation, the forests of Vega Prime seemed to ebb and flow with life. Deep woods bled into ranges of black mountains scarred by pockets of incredible rock formations and bizarre symmetrical outcroppings. Within the recesses were flickers of small movements, hidden things, and unknown creatures.

Thousands of feet below, a marsh-like swamp teemed with bizarre insect-like creatures and acrid smells.

In a clearing deep within the foul bog lay an object of such immeasurable beauty that it seemed foreign to the rest of the unsightly surroundings. The massive crystal-like sculpture stretched toward the sky with weaving flames of clear resin that joined in its center.

Trapped within the holocaust of symbolic fire was a human man's carved glass form, his hands reaching toward the heavens. The statue's crystal face contorted with agony; its mouth gaped in a silent scream.

* * *

ALSO BY
PAUL J. SALAMOFF

Graphic Novels

Hired Guns

Tales of Discord

Discord

Logan's Run: Rebirth

Logan's Run: Aftermath

Logan's Run: Last Day

Presidential Pets: The History of Pets In The White House

Orbit: The Cast of Doctor Who

Roger Corman's Black Scorpion

Nonfiction

On The Set: The Hidden Rules of Movie Making Etiquette

Short Fiction

Tamara

(From the anthology *Midian Unmade: Tales of Clive Barker's Nightbreed*)

Bad Fix

(From the anthology *Hell Comes To Hollywood*)

Can You Imagine...

(From the anthology *The Devil's Coattails*)

ABOUT THE AUTHOR

Paul J. Salamoff

 Paul J. Salamoff has worked for over 30 years in film, TV, video games, and graphic novels as a writer, producer, director, executive, and make-up f/x artist.

He is the author of "On the Set: The Hidden Rules of Movie Making Etiquette"; the graphic novels "Hired Guns", "Discord", and "Logan's Run". His short stories and essays have appeared in anthologies, including "Midian Unmade: Tales from Clive Barker's Nightbreed" and "The Cyberpunk Nexus: Exploring the Blade Runner Universe".

Paul currently teaches screenwriting at New York Film Academy. He is a two-time Bram Stoker Award nominee who made his feature-film directorial debut in 2019 with Encounter, a science fiction drama based on his original screenplay, which won Best Independent Film at the 46th annual Saturn Awards.

ABOUT THE AUTHOR

Oren Nichols

Oren Nichols is a lifelong writer who has worked in diverse fields such as entertainment and technology to support his passion. Honing his skills first as a writer's assistant and editor and then as a technology analyst, he made the leap to full-time writer in 2023 at the behest of colleagues. Oren's previous work was primarily behind-the-scenes or in settings where anonymity is the default.

He is currently working on several novels and screenplays, solo and with collaborators, in varying stages of development.

Oren lives in rural New York with his two dogs, Turbo and Greasemonkey, and a roommate who wishes to remain anonymous so the greys don't find him. His hobbies include video games, high-end audio, and restoring historical photographs and film footage.

CONNECT
REACH OUT TO THE AUTHORS

PAUL J. SALAMOFF
www.paulsalamoff.com
tavinpress@gmail.com

OREN NICHOLS
www.orennichols.com
orennicholsauthor@gmail.com

TAVIN PRESS
www.tavinpress.com

29377875R10115